DRAGON RACER

THE SILVER FLAME

DRAGON RACER

THE SILVER FLAME

Margaret Bateson-Hill

Catnip

CATNIP BOOKS
Published by Catnip Publishing Ltd
Quality Court, off Chancery Lane
London WC2A 1HR

First published 2014
1 3 5 7 9 10 8 6 4 2

Text © 2014 Margaret Bateson-Hill
The moral right of the author has been asserted.

A CIP catalogue record for this book is available from the British Library.

ISBN 978-1-84647-1742

Printed in Poland

www.catnippublishing.co.uk

To Kathryn Chorley – for suggesting Amber

*And the fire shall try every man's worth,
of what sort it is.*

1 Corinthians 3:13

CONTENTS

PROLOGUE

Long black shadows were moving over the sand, strangely white in the bright moonlight. Faces were hidden, but all wore the same edgy, excited look. The small band was bonded forever now, knowing they had run a terrible risk. But, oh how the night would stay with them. They'd never forget the ripping of dragon wing, the explosion of fire and smoke, the hard crack of a dragon's broken skull. It had been a fight to the finish. Already the ocean waves were washing away the black pool of dragon blood. In the morning the beach would look exactly the same as it always had. No clue as to the deadly secret they had witnessed that very evening. Even as the group made its way up the steep path away from the beach, the members knew it was not the physical effort of climbing that drove their racing heartbeats.

Cliff Heywood waited on the cliff top, hidden behind the darkened windows of his Lexus, until the last of his visitors had driven away into the night. When all was still and quiet, he took out his phone.

'Dr Braithwaite,' he drawled in his easy West Coast accent. 'So sorry you couldn't join us this evening. But just wait till you see the recording – it's gonna take your breath away.'

Cliff got out of his car and walked slowly over to the cliff edge. The ocean was lost in the darkness below, but he could hear waves pounding the rocks. High tide. And this was a high tide moment for Cliff – just a couple of months to go before his twenty-eighth birthday and he was *still* helping out his dad with the family business. He was practically managing the place and yet getting paid next to nothing. Tired of the 'one day all this will be yours' argument, Cliff had come up with a venture of his own. But he needed a backer – a *rich* backer – and his sources informed him that this Dr Braithwaite was a very interested party.

'Dr Braithwaite' probably wasn't his real name, of course. The thrill of an illegal fight club went hand in hand with anonymity. Cliff imagined him as some bored businessman, past his prime and with too much money. At this very moment he would be clicking on the video attachment in the email Cliff had sent him. Cliff smiled, imagining his investor watching as the doors of two transporter vans slid slowly open and the silhouettes of two dark shapes emerged from the darkness . . .

Dr Braithwaite's eyes were fixed on the screen, unable to look away, and the hairs on the back of his neck prickled as a blood-curdling roar exploded from the computer.

He watched, mesmerised, until the screen went blank. Still he didn't move, but sat there reliving every moment – every thrust and kick and bite. Slowly a smile spread across his face and he picked up the phone.

I
SPEED!

*Independence Day Speed Trials and World
Championship Race*

July 4th, San Francisco

Joanna Morris zipped up her racing jacket, tightened the strap on her helmet, and pulled on her racing gloves. But instead of climbing on to her silver dragon, Excelsior, as the racing official was expecting, she stood beside him, her hand gently resting on his back.

'Ms Morris, is there a problem?' The official was looking concerned and unsure what to say next to the young teenage racer. 'The race? The World Championship final. It's about to start.'

Joanna ignored him, just as she was ignoring the

growing roar of spectators outside the dragon cave and the thumping of her own heart.

She had promised herself and Excelsior this moment before the final race – just a moment to remember all the dragons that had died earlier that season, killed by the terrible flu virus – and to express her eternal gratitude that Excelsior had survived.

'Ms Morris, I must insist!' The official came and tapped Joanna on the shoulder. To his relief she finally climbed on to her dragon in preparation to race. As soon as the official had gone, Excelsior turned to Joanna.

'So, how much do you think we'll win by?'

Joanna reached up to her helmet and turned on the small camera that would relay the race back to the giant screens in the stadium, where the race would finish.

'Feeling confident then, XL?' She grinned broadly at her dragon. Joanna loved that Excelsior never doubted his own ability.

The silver dragon quivered with excitement. 'Today I will fly faster than any dragon ever before. Are you ready for that JoJo Dragon Flyer?'

Joanna's response was to ask the mind-blend questions that allowed her and XL to share their thoughts – to think and race as one.

What are you?

I am a dragon
What is your name?
My name is Excelsior
What type of dragon are you?
I'm Silver Spiked-Back
Shall we mind-blend?
Yes

Excelsior's thoughts whirled through Joanna's mind. She felt the bright heat of fire spinning in his belly, the trembling of his wings ready to unfurl, the tense contraction of muscles in his hind legs ready to launch them skyward . . .

There were seconds to go now before the starting siren. Outside the cave the spectators in the stands had fallen silent. Everyone was waiting.

Two remaining teams. One final elimination race. Winner takes all. Brixton, UK versus New York Central, USA.

On Joanna's command to *FLY!* Excelsior exploded out of the starting cave and up into the air. On the far side of the racecourse their rivals had got off to an equally fast start, but the wind direction was currently in Excelsior's favour and he was already taking full advantage.

'Ready to *race our way into the record books?*' he roared excitedly as he adjusted the angle of his wings and started to spin the fire in his belly, hotter and faster, so that they could 'curl' – a technique they had devised earlier in the season to exploit the power of Excelsior's fire and turn it into speed.

Deep within the mind-blend Joanna felt spinning flames curl around her, allowing her to ride down the great curves of hot fire like a surfer riding a wave. To the spectators below they were little more than a thin glimmer of silver streaking in and out of the clouds.

They quickly left the city behind them. Rocks and trees replaced buildings, whilst away to the right was the never-ending ocean. Joanna and Excelsior were out in front, but their rivals were putting up a valiant challenge and purposely disappeared into a particularly thick bank of cloud so the Brixton team would be left guessing their position.

Joanna tried to track them. Immediately, she felt their mind-block. That was expected, but what took her completely by surprise was an angry twist of red fire that flashed through her mind. Joanna cried out loud as though she had been physically hit.

'What was that? Mind-blocks don't feel like that. I must have disturbed some other dragon in a cave below.'

'I'm not staying round to find out,' said Excelsior. They had little time to think any more about the twisted red fire, as they caught sight of their American rivals giving chase behind them. For one moment

Joanna feared they would be caught. Concentrating all her thoughts she willed Excelsior to spin the fire in his belly faster still.

He rocketed forward and, before Joanna knew it, Excelsior was preparing to land; buildings grew tall, people had faces. She felt a heavy thud as his silver claws snatched the ground in the middle of the landing strip. Only once they had come to a complete standstill did Joanna allow her thoughts to separate from her dragon's. She sat there for a moment, relief flooding through her. They were still World Champions! But winning the race wasn't enough for her dragon. She turned her attention back to the question preoccupying him – how fast had they flown?

A crowd of officials were running to and fro and conferring on walkie-talkies. A few more seconds . . . and the news exploded on to the screens:

A NEW WORLD RECORD TIME
10 minutes 2.075 seconds

'YES!' cried Joanna, jumping down from the dragon excitedly. 'XL, we did it!'

She looked across at her trainer. Spiky Mike gave her a very big thumbs-up. Next to him, her friends Mouse and Dominic were leaping and cheering wildly. Where was Isaac? He was the person who'd made this race possible. Isaac had learned to make the silver fire of alchemy and saved Excelsior from the virus that should have killed him. Funny to think she used to hate him so much, when now she couldn't imagine life in the caves without her friend.

There he was, standing slightly to one side and checking the race data on the big screen. Joanna waved over to him and he waved back. She was about to go over to talk to him when she heard a sudden blast of trumpet over the loudspeaker announcing the trophy presentation. The newly appointed president of the World Dragon Racing Federation and countless other WDRF representatives were already making their way in solemn procession to the centre of the stadium. They carried flowers, runners-up medals and, of course, the great silver World Championship Cup and Speed Record Shield. But what surprised and delighted Joanna the most was seeing see that the new president was none other than Marion Claverdale, former World Champion and mother to her fellow Brixton flyer, Hannibal Henry Oliver.

Joanna climbed on to the winner's podium to accept the shield and cup. With a great sense of pride she lifted first the great silver cup and then the speed-record shield up into the air, before turning to face the one remaining flag flying in the stadium – that of her own Brixton Caves, with its silver star on its field of black and gold as they played the British National Anthem.

'For you Vincent,' she said quietly. It was already seventeen months since his death, yet Joanna still felt the loss of the man to whom she owed everything.

As Joanna climbed down from the podium she looked over at Excelsior. There was a man standing by the dragon's side with a great syringe in his hand. He was looking round furtively, with his head down, so she couldn't see his face. Did she know him? What was he doing?

Joanna's blood ran cold. Instantly she was back in the cave in Brighton, when her arch-enemy, Marius King, had ordered Excelsior to be injected with the flu virus. It couldn't be HIM, not here – could it? She ran and hurled herself against the man, pushing him to the ground.

2
FRIENDS AT
A BARBECUE

'Get off! Don't you dare touch my dragon!' Joanna pounded the man with her fists.

Immediately security surrounded them. Spiky Mike came rushing over and pulled Joanna off.

'It's Marius King,' screamed Joanna. 'He's trying to kill Excelsior. I saw him inject him . . .'

Spiky Mike looked at the man now handcuffed to two burly security men.

'It's just a WDRF vet coming to take a routine doping sample.'

'What?' Joanna looked aghast at the poor man, who was, understandably, looking at Joanna with some trepidation. 'I thought it was Marius King coming to attack Excelsior. Oh I'm sorry, I'm so sorry.'

Fortunately Marion Claverdale came to the rescue.

'Joanna has had not only an emotionally and

physically exhausting day, but a whole season. I'm sure Donald,' she smiled at the WDRF vet, 'quite understands it was just a misunderstanding. I think in this case the testing can take place back in the dragon caves. As for our young champion here, it's time I reciprocated the hospitality the UK has shown to my son. I'd like to show Jo how we celebrate this side of the Atlantic by inviting her to a special Independence Day barbecue.'

'I'll take Excelsior back to his cave,' said Spiky Mike to a still distressed Joanna. 'Look, Dominic's waiting to congratulate you.'

Joanna blushed as Dominic pushed his way through a sea of reporters, aware they'd all be wanting to know who the good-looking boy was. He picked up her winner's bouquet in one hand and flung his arm around her shoulder. Conscious that cameras were clicking all around her, Joanna walked quickly on, announcing loudly,

'Let's go and find the others.'

'I *really* thought it was Marius King,' said Joanna to her friends. They were sitting round a huge table laden with buckets of ribs, burgers, hotdogs and fries. Joanna was happily squashed between Dominic and her best friend Mouse – both trying to outdo the other in celebrating their friend's victory. Mouse picked up a handful of popcorn and expertly tossed pieces up into the air and caught them in her mouth.

'We were all getting ready to leap over the barrier and come and help you. It was the vet's fault, creeping up on Excelsior like that.'

'Who cares about creepy vets?' exclaimed Dominic. A huge grin spread across his face. 'When you've just broken your own world record!'

Dominic and Mouse whooped and cheered and started dancing round the table, in the process spilling a great deal of iced tea everywhere and drenching themselves so completely that they had to go and ask a helpful steward to find them some towels.

Isaac looked across at Joanna. He was smiling, but his dark eyes looked serious.

'The final race was awesome – final proof that Excelsior hasn't suffered any long-term side effects from the flu.'

Joanna nodded. 'Thanks to you. I can never thank you enough for saving him. I think about it all the time, you know – how you made the silver fire . . . and about Marius King.' She tried to stop her voice from shaking.

Isaac leant forward. 'Are you OK?'

There was no point lying, not to Isaac.

'I couldn't see his face. And it's just the sort of thing Marius King would do . . .' She shuddered.

'I know he's still out to get me. Me *and* Excelsior. I sometimes lie awake wondering where he is. He'll have been watching today. I know it.'

The celebration finished with a great firework display, but Joanna insisted on checking on Excelsior before they went back to the hotel. Security weren't too pleased, but they could hardly refuse the world champion. The 'caves' for the World Championships were state of the art – temperature and light regulated, with CCTV security and coded entry. They would have to be accompanied by a security guard. As they waited for the lift to take them to the caves, Joanna realised she'd left her winner's bouquet back at the barbeque. Mouse looked pointedly at Dominic to suggest he volunteer to go back and get it, but he shrugged his shoulders.

'It could be anywhere.'

Mouse sighed! Another opportunity for Dominic to show Joanna he 'liked' her and as usual he missed it.

'It's by the table with the trophies,' said Isaac. 'I remember seeing it.

'Would you mind getting it for me, whilst I check XL?' asked Joanna apologetically. Isaac hurried back to the barbecue. He found Joanna's bouquet easily enough, but it was all squashed and falling apart and a card had been shoved into the flowers at the top. He pulled it out and opened it. It had a black border and fancy writing printed across the middle.

Till we meet again.

It looked just like the funeral cards his grandma had got when his grandpa died. But who would send Jo a funeral card? Was it some kind of sick joke? Or, together with the trashed flowers, was it a threat? Remembering Joanna's fears, his thoughts leapt immediately to Marius King.

Isaac ran over to where Marion Claverdale was talking to one of her guests. She looked up when she saw him.

'Can I help you? I think your friends have gone to visit Excelsior.'

Isaac suddenly found himself tongue-tied. He was letting his imagination get the better of him. How could an escaped convict, wanted by Interpol, get into the country, let alone be at the World Championship? The flowers could easily have been stepped on, or squashed accidentally. And the card was probably from a fan that had met Jo at some race or other and hoped to meet her again.

'Nothing, Ms Claverdale,' Isaac said. 'Just wanted to congratulate you on your appointment. Thanks for a great evening.'

Isaac ripped the card into tiny pieces and dropped them in a bin and left the flowers on the table. He'd just have to tell Joanna that he couldn't find them.

3
A FANTASTIC OFFER

From: admin@t&c_enterprises.com
To: Adam Braithwaite

Dear Doctor Braithwaite,

For an investment of $500,000 Tooth and Claw Enterprises to provide dragons for three dragon fights

The fight clubs to take place on dates to be decided by mutual agreement.

Attendance by invitation only at a cost of $10,000, of which Tooth and Claw Enterprises will take a 30% cut.

Regards,

Cliff

From: Adam Braithwaite
To: admin@t&c_enterprises.com

ALL my fights will take place in the UK.

For the first two fights I require fighting dragons with good form – tantalising appetisers to drum up interest for my third and final fight, to be billed as 'Grand Finale'.

For this fight Tooth and Claw Enterprises will provide one fully-grown Jewel Dragon.

As for its opponent, you needn't concern yourself with that. I have my eye on something very special...

Accept and I double my investment to one million dollars.

Dr Braithwaite

Cliff reread the email for the fifth time. One million dollars! It was a fantastic offer. With that sort of money he could start up a whole string of fight clubs across the States. Moving Braithwaite's fights to the UK wasn't a problem. He'd already eyed up the UK market and had contacts ready and willing, just waiting for the green light.

But a mature Jewel Dragon! Even in an illegal world of dragon fight clubs, where rules were few and far between, people steered clear of Jewel Dragons. Their reputation for viciousness was legendary.

He hesitated for one brief moment . . . then picked up the phone.

One phone call later and Cliff Heywood could only wonder what he had got himself into. There was a manic quality about Braithwaite that made his blood run cold. It wasn't his desire for financial gain or love of power . . . No, some other motivation was driving this man. Something dark, violent and deadly.

All of a sudden acquiring one Jewel Dragon seemed the least of his problems.

4
THE DEVIL'S
SLIDE CAVES

Joanna awoke suddenly and sat up. The clock next to her bed said three o'clock. She lay back on the pillow, hoping she'd get back to sleep quickly, but her brain was buzzing with too many thoughts. All week she'd thought about little else but the race and now everything was crowding back in. First thing in the morning she was going to be interviewed on some prime-time sports TV programme. She always enjoyed interviews where she could talk about racing and Excelsior, but recently interviewers had started asking about her friendship with Dominic. She always answered they were just good friends. The trouble was she didn't really know the answer herself anymore. She had to admit when she first met him she did fancy him – he was very good-looking, and he was the only other person her age that raced. But that was before . . . before she got to know Isaac properly. Ever since she'd seen him in a mind-blend with Excelsior, when he saved her dragon's life with the Silver Flame, she'd come to see him differently and to trust him more. Not that she'd ever told anyone this, not even Mouse. She could hear Mouse's slow soft breathing in the bed on the other side of the room. Mouse, who made everything fun and larked around with everyone. Yes, she'd stick close to Mouse and keep all her feelings to herself.

Joanna must have fallen asleep again without realising it because when she opened her eyes it was bright sunshine and Mouse was singing (loudly) in the shower, '*We are the Champions!*'

Joanna leapt out of bed and knocked loudly on the bathroom door.

'Not the champions of singing!' she called.

Seconds later Mouse appeared wrapped up in a huge hotel dressing gown, ferociously rubbing her hair dry with a towel.

'No one appreciates my singing talent – hey did you know you called out in your sleep last night? '

'Did I?' asked Joanna, nervously, recalling her own thoughts. 'What did I shout?'

'It sounded like '*gotcha*'. Perhaps you were dreaming that Dominic was chasing you?'

Mouse gave a questioning smile. She was as

desperate as anyone else to know what her friend *really* thought of Dominic.

Joanna shook her head.

'No, I wasn't and don't joke – I've got this TV interview later this morning and I certainly don't want questions like that!'

'Just make something up,' suggested Mouse. 'Say that Spiky Mike has forbidden any boyfriends until your sixteenth birthday because nothing must come in the way of your training.'

Joanna laughed. She could imagine Spiky Mike saying just that.

'Brilliant! You should be my publicist!' said Joanna. *And if* I *can keep my feelings about Dominic and Isaac secret from* you *then no one else should guess either*, she added silently

Thanks to Mouse's coaching Joanna sailed through the probing questions of the TV interviewer, leaving two spectators rather bemused.

'I didn't say anything of the kind!' insisted Spiky Mike to Afra, his fiancée and rival Brixton trainer, as they watched on the monitor.

'Tell *him* that then,' said Afra, indicating a rather crestfallen Dominic.

Spiky Mike shook his head, horrified.

'I can't – he'd be totally embarrassed.'

Afra smiled to herself, knowing it was more a question of her fiancé's embarrassment. And possibly why he suddenly seemed very interested in watching the autocue.

'Lunch, everyone!' said Spiky Mike hastily as soon as Joanna came off the set. All this teenager stuff was more than he could deal with and feeding them seemed a good answer to most crises.

Over lunch Spiky Mike suggested they all drive out to visit a huge dragon caves consortium as time was running out for both Hannibal and Dominic if they were to find new dragons to race in the coming season.

The journey to the caves took them out along the Pacific coast and Joanna was more than content to stare out of the window and watch the waves crashing to the shore whilst she listened to Hannibal and Dominic discussing the perfect dragon. They were both so hopeful, and yet . . . could you just *choose* a dragon, like shopping for a new dress? She couldn't imagine it and yet it *could* so easily have been her. What would she have done if Excelsior *had* died? Poor Hannibal had lost not one, but *two* dragons – though surely that brute Prometheus didn't count. She shuddered just thinking about the ferocious Jewel dragon, who had nearly destroyed them all. Who *had* killed Vincent . . .

'What's this place we're going to?' she asked Spiky Mike quickly.

'Afra's got a brochure if you want to see,' he replied. 'It's called the Devil's Slide Caves, but it's more of a complex on top of the cliffs with a series of man-made caves for viewing the dragons.'

The brochure showed glossy photos of shiny laboratories for hatching dragon eggs, a spectacular flying field and, of course, the dragon caves. There were also photographs of dragons who'd been sold alongside glowing testimonials and a list of the races they'd won.

'So this is more of a massive dragon breeding place?' asked Joanna.

'Most cave owners don't like the hassle and expense of employing an egg-turner.' said Spiky Mike. 'And of course you get to see the dragon before you buy it. They can offer a huge number of breeds. The US champion Sundance Kid that you raced against in the quarter finals – he was from here.'

'How many egg-turners are there?' asked Isaac, who'd been listening intently to the conversation.

'Says a team of five,' said Joanna, reading through the brochure.

'And do they turn their own eggs or does everyone just muck in? I mean, it's not very personal. How do you get to know the egg and sense what it needs? Grandma's been teaching me how to observe the shifting weight as the dragon develops and how to adjust the position of the egg to make sure you get an even distribution of heat . . .' He let his voice trail away, surprised at his own outburst.

'Bit technical for me,' grimaced Dominic. 'As long as the dragon is fast I don't really care if it's had one egg-turner or fifty.'

'It's the attention to small detail that makes all the difference,' insisted Isaac.

Joanna thought he sounded angry.

Dominic didn't seem to notice.

'What about the egg at the Brixton caves? My grandma gave you it for free, so can I have that one when it's born? ' He turned to Joanna hopefully.

'Sorry Dominic, if Hannibal hasn't found a dragon by then he must be offered it first,' said Joanna.

'It's not due to hatch until mid-October,' Spiky Mike butted in. 'So anyone who wants to fly this season needs to find a dragon now. But Joanna is right – Hannibal would be given first refusal.'

'I can see I'm going to be left with everyone else's rejects,' said Dominic, turning away, only half-joking.

'Hey man,' said Hannibal, ever the peacemaker. 'Let's just see what we find today. Perhaps we'll get lucky like Jo and an amazing dragon will choose one of us as its flyer.'

The Devil's Slide Caves were in the most spectacular setting, high on the cliffs overlooking a long coastline of wild Pacific Ocean. Spiky Mike followed the sign-posted road round to a parking lot in front of a series of modern white buildings set amongst cultivated green lawns. A man with shoulder-length blond hair was waiting to meet them. He was tall and well built, casually dressed in jeans and checked shirt and aviator sunglasses.

'Hi, guys, I'm Cliff. Glad you dropped by to check us out. Don't suppose you have anything on this scale in the UK?'

Hannibal came over and gave Cliff a high five. 'That's why we're here. So where are the dragons?"

Cliff laughed and pointed to a shiny glass elevator. 'Four at a time, if you don't mind.'

Spiky Mike, Afra and Hannibal followed him.

'Hurry up Dominic,' called Spiky Mike.

'I thought I'd go with the others,' said Dominic. He was standing back slightly, with his hands stuffed in his jeans and his dark hair flopping forward.

'I'll go,' said Isaac, walking forward. But Spiky Mike stopped him.

'Dominic, are you serious about finding a dragon? Because we are running out of possibilities. Get in the lift NOW!'

Dominic slouched into the lift.

'See you in a minute,' Joanna called after him.

They found Dominic leaning against a rock outside the entrance to the caves.

'Go and see the amazing dragon then, I told you I'd only get second choice.'

Mouse and Isaac went on ahead, but Joanna stayed with Dominic.

'What's the matter, Dominic?' She tried to sound concerned, even though she was desperate to follow the others.

Dominic shrugged his shoulders. 'She's a jet black Nebula called Ebony. Hannibal's going to give her a trial flight. They didn't even ask me if I wanted a go.'

'Have you looked at any other dragons?' asked Joanna cautiously. Dominic scowled.

'Nothing like Ebony. *Your* trainer says there's a Scarlet Spiked-Back in there that would be perfect for me. I was hoping for something more exciting.'

'Spiky Mike tends to be right about dragons,' said Joanna, putting her hand on his shoulder.

Dominic shrugged her off. 'Don't be patronising, Jo.'

Joanna was furious. 'I was trying to be nice.'

'Have to *try*, do you?' he replied scornfully.

Joanna decided Dominic was better left to snap out of his mood on his own and went to find the others. She bumped into them almost immediately. Mouse's eyes were shining.

'Jo, she is GORGEOUS. We're going to a viewing balcony to watch Hannibal fly her – come on.'

Joanna could only stare in amazement as the handler led Ebony from the cave. Without a doubt – whatever her feelings for Excelsior – Ebony was the most beautiful dragon Joanna had ever seen. She was a deep midnight black; her small scales making her look extra sleek and shiny. A ridge of small fine spikes flowed down her back. On the top of her head there was a silver crest that matched perfectly a pair of bright sparkling silver eyes. Joanna was desperate to see her wings, but they were tightly held against her sides. Everything about this streamlined dragon said fast. No wonder Dominic was feeling put out.

Well XL, thought Joanna. *What will you make of Ebony?*

Spiky Mike must have been thinking the same thing. 'Impressive, don't you think?'

'Stunning,' admitted Joanna.

Hannibal went straight over to the dragon, and climbed on. With a sudden sweep Ebony took to the skies. Out over the ocean they flew, soaring high up into the clouds, only to reappear in a different part of the sky in a downward spiral. As she watched them Joanna suddenly wondered what it would be like to lose . . .

5
MEET THE
PENHALIGONS

It was the best possible outcome. Hannibal was besotted by Ebony, calling her the most perfect dragon ever, and now all that needed to be done was the paperwork. Cliff led them through to an office with a huge panoramic window looking out over the ocean. Hannibal and Afra were halfway through signing the documents when there was a knock and a man stuck his head round the door.

'Sorry Cli— er, Mr Heywood, didn't realise you had visit—' He suddenly broke off and stepped into the room.

'I don't believe it. Afra? How lovely to see you.'

Afra stood up immediately and went to hug him.

'Jamie? What a surprise. I didn't know you were working here.'

'It's Doctor Penhaligon now, if you don't mind,' he laughed. 'I qualified last year.'

Afra turned towards Spiky Mike with a rather self-conscious smile.

'Mike – it's Jamie!'

Spiky Mike nodded unenthusiastically. 'I can see that.'

'So what are you doing at Devil's Slide?' Jamie asked Afra, ignoring Spiky Mike.

'We've just gone and bought the Black Nebula for Hannibal. Hannibal – come and meet an old friend of mine, Jamie Penhaligon.'

Jamie shook Hannibal warmly by the hand.

'Got yourself not just the best dragon in these caves, but also the best trainer I know.'

Afra shook her head.

'Actually, that honour belongs to my fiancé.'

Jamie looked Spiky Mike slowly up and down.

'Fiancé? I suppose I should say congratulations.' He turned back to Afra and winked. 'Guess that was my own fault for coming to study in the States.'

Joanna, who'd been staring out of the window, was suddenly all attention. Jamie Penhaligon was an old friend of Afra's? From the conversation and looks Joanna wondered just *how* friendly. She could feel Mouse nudging her in the back, obviously thinking the same thing.

Joanna looked again at Jamie. Not a hair out of place, clean-shaven, smartly dressed in designer chinos, polo shirt, and polished shoes. Pretty much the opposite of Spiky Mike, who was, as always, dressed in jeans and a scruffy T-shirt.

Out of loyalty to her trainer Joanna instantly decided Jamie Penhaligon was a little too smooth and perfect. She went and stood protectively by Spiky Mike's side.

'And this young lady I recognise as World Champion,' said Jamie with a smile. 'The Devil's Slide Caves are flattered!'

Joanna smiled back angelically. 'It's as Afra said, I have the *best* trainer.'

Jamie was all smiles. 'I'll be part of the action myself next season. I'm coming back to the UK to work for the WDRF, with special responsibility for all new dragons flying next season. Ebony will be under my supervision.' He turned to Cliff. 'I was just coming to let you know that I'm increasing Geronimo's sedation. He's been very restless all day.'

As Jamie was about to leave, Mouse suggested it was time they looked for Dominic. The vet offered to show Joanna, Isaac and Mouse where to find him.

'Probably talking to Amber.'

Joanna glanced at Mouse who shrugged. She didn't know who Amber was either.

Jamie pointed to a cave where Dominic was standing, discussing the Scarlet Spiked-Back dragon with a girl. Much to Joanna's relief he was smiling – then she realised he was smiling at the girl, not at the dragon.

'Is Amber the girl or the dragon?' hissed Mouse.

Joanna looked more carefully at the girl. She was about her own age, tall and wearing skinny jeans. She had long strawberry blond hair and was seriously pretty. Dominic certainly seemed to think so – he didn't even glance round when Joanna called out. Joanna was annoyed with herself for minding. Was she jealous?

'See, your friends haven't forgotten you after all, Dominic,' said the girl. 'But you didn't say one of them was World Champion.' The girl turned to Joanna. 'Congratulations! That was *amazing* yesterday. Dominic – introduce us.'

Dominic turned rather sheepishly to face the others. 'This is Amber Penhaligon . . .'

'Amber Penhaligon?' interrupted Joanna. 'So Jamie is . . .'

'My brother. He's completely the best big brother ever. He works too hard, though.' Amber flicked her hair and smiled at them all. 'I know you're Joanna Morris, so I'm presuming you're Mouse . . .' Amber smiled quickly at Mouse, who looked rather pleased that Amber knew who she was, before turning to Isaac.

'Are you Isaac Ankama, who saved all those dragons from last year's flu thing?'

Joanna was suddenly aware that Amber was touching Isaac on his arm and that he didn't move away. He shrugged his shoulders and smiled.

'Yes, that's me.'

'Do you fly?' Joanna asked quickly, feeling the need to say something . . . anything.

'Grew up flying! My dad owns these really old Cornish dragon caves.' Amber flicked her hair again. 'Not that he'll let me race. It's so unfair! And we've got this perfect Scarlet Spiked-Back dragon, like the one here, just waiting to be raced.'

'Perhaps I could buy it?' said Dominic excitedly. 'Do you think Spiky Mike would take me down to see before I go home to South Africa for the summer?' Joanna noticed that although he was talking to her it was Amber he was looking at.

In fact both Isaac and Dominic were grinning at Amber like Cheshire cats.

Not knowing if Dominic really wanted an answer to his question, Jo stood there just looking at him. Then without warning an intense stab of pain flashed through her head. She grabbed hold of Dominic, barely able to stand.

'I . . . help me . . .' she called. Hands all around her were trying to hold her up, but the pain was growing, pulsing through her brain. Her legs gave way beneath her and she fell into darkness.

Joanna woke up in a room she didn't recognise. It was dark and all she could see was the whiteness of the sheets on the thin bed she was lying on. Why was she here? She remembered being in the cave and talking with Dominic and that girl with the long, flicky hair . . . Amber. Then from out of nowhere had come this blinding pain. Joanna swallowed hard. She could feel how tense she was. Her heart was pounding in her chest and her pulse was racing.

A dark figure suddenly moved on the other side of the room and she screamed.

'Joanna?' came a man's voice she didn't recognise. 'It's Dr Penhaligon. You fainted. Just lie still. Probably a reaction to all the excitement of winning yesterday.'

Joanna didn't speak. Surging through the pain she'd felt the burning fury of dark red flame twisting round and round upon itself – the same fire she'd experienced the day before, only much stronger. Had she flown over these caves in yesterday's race? She was always susceptible to picking up a dragon's thoughts – especially a dragon in distress, only this was something more than an ill or injured dragon.

Cautiously she concentrated her thoughts on the memory of the dark red flame and asked the first of the mind-blend questions that she always asked when she wanted to make personal contact with a dragon.

What are you?

There was no reply, just a wall of silence. She was vaguely aware of the chatter of other dragons close by in the background, but it was as though they were talking in whispers. She opened her thoughts to them, asking who the dragon in pain was, but one by one they closed their minds off.

She sat up in the bed.

'Dr Penhaligon, the dragon you mentioned earlier this afternoon, the sedated one, is he or she in a lot of pain?'

'Yes,' smiled Dr Penhaligon, 'But on the mend now.'

'What was the matter?' asked Joanna.

'Got in a scrap with another dragon,' said Jamie. 'A bit of boisterous fun that got out of hand. Now, if you're feeling better shall we go and find your friends? They're with Amber.'

Joanna followed Jamie across the greenest lawn she'd ever seen to an apartment block. As they got nearer she saw her friends sitting round the edge of a large outdoor pool.

It was Mouse who caught sight of Joanna first. She came running over.

'Are you OK? I wasn't allowed to stay with you.'

'I'm fine, but I'll tell you more later, in private. Are Spiky Mike and Afra here?'

'No,' said Mouse. 'I thought they'd be with you.'

Joanna stared angrily at Dr Penhaligon. 'Haven't you told them I fainted?'

Jamie looked rather amused at Joanna's outburst. 'Calm down. I'll phone Cliff's office now. Instead of getting yourself all worked up, why not have some orange juice or iced tea?'

The girls took their drinks over to the pool. Joanna was still too upset to notice Mouse getting equally agitated until her friend suddenly burst out, 'Oh those two need pushing in at the deep end. Anyone would think they'd never seen someone swim before.'

Joanna looked at her friend, bewildered. 'What are you talking about?'

Mouse shrugged her shoulders. 'Look at the pair of them!'

It was only then that Joanna realised that Dominic and Isaac were standing, enthralled, watching Amber dive from a low board.

'I mean Dominic could at least come over and see how you are,' said Mouse furiously. 'Amber's been flirting with both of them the whole time.'

Joanna looked across at her friends. Dominic's lack of concern didn't upset her, but it was a shock to see the look of admiration on Isaac's face.

Things didn't get any better when the other three turned up a few minutes later. Spiky Mike was furious when he saw Jamie.

'What are you playing at, Penhaligon, not telling me that Joanna had fainted the moment it happened? Jo, are you OK?'

'Sorry – didn't realise it was that big a deal. She was only out for a few minutes,' said Jamie, shrugging off Spiky Mike's outburst. 'I thought the pool would be a nicer place for them all to wait whilst you finished off your business. Look, none of you've had a chance to relax after the races, so why doesn't everyone have a swim and I'll get the barbecue going? Hey, Afra – do you remember *that* barbecue we had up in Scotland, after your first race?'

Joanna thought for a moment that Spiky Mike might actually hit Jamie. Afra was certainly looking flustered and embarrassed.

'Another time perhaps, Jamie,' she said. 'We need to be getting back.'

The journey back was silent. Joanna wished she could eavesdrop on her friends' thoughts the way she could with dragons. With the exception of Hannibal, who was obviously thinking of his new dragon, she imagined everyone else was rather preoccupied with one or other of the Penhaligons.

6
BACK
HOME

It was a relief to get back to Brixton. With Hannibal and Afra staying behind to oversee Ebony's transfer, it had been a fraught journey home with Spiky Mike responsible for the four teenagers. When they landed, they'd said goodbye to Dominic, whose grandmother had picked him up to take him to Suffolk for a stopover before he flew back to South Africa for the rest of the summer. It had been a nice enough goodbye, but Joanna was more than relieved she could ignore the whole boyfriend/ friend thing for a few weeks at least.

Agnes, the old egg-turner, and Joanna's tutor, Mr Hogan, were both waiting down in the Brixton Caves to welcome them all and to admire the trophies as they were placed back in the trophy cabinet for another year.

'That final race, when you broke the World Record,' applauded Mr Hogan. 'I was watching it with some friends of mine and I nearly burst with pride when one of them commented that it was the best bit of flying she'd ever seen.'

'I've saved all the newspapers for you, Joanna,' smiled Agnes. 'You were headline news.'

Of course they wanted to congratulate her and Joanna thanked them both, hoping now they'd let her settle back into life at the caves without too much fuss. She gave Agnes a quick hug, saying she'd read the papers after she'd checked on Excelsior.

The two girls hurried down to Excelsior's cave. Joanna stopped for a moment by the old heavy wooden door. She always loved this moment, seeing the first shimmer of silver stretched out in the centre of the cave and the shadows of his spiked back reaching up the wall. How she thought he was lying so still that he must be asleep, only to see the tiny curl of smoke from his nostrils and a glimmer of fiery eyes escaping from under his eyelids so that she knew he'd been watching the whole time. She made Mouse wait with her in the doorway.

'I think he's asleep,' giggled Mouse as they slipped inside the cave. 'He's snoring!'

'I am not snoring,' growled XL under his breath. 'Just slightly jetlagged. There was this crazy Golden

Flame dragon from France in the berth next to mine and she would not shut up. And I could do with a slight snack – it might be four in the afternoon for you lot, but my stomach says breakfast.'

As if on cue the door opened and in came Isaac with a bucket of chicken livers.

'Thought XL would want something to eat,' was all he said.

'Now I know I'm home,' said Excelsior with a satisfied sigh. 'That US food was OK, but nothing like a bucket of English chicken livers!'

Joanna and Mouse chatted excitedly about being back in Brixton, but Isaac seemed rather distracted and stood silently watching Excelsior munch his way through his meal. As soon as Excelsior had finished he picked up the bucket and left the cave without saying a word.

'See you at the egg-turning,' Joanna called after him, but she wasn't sure he heard. Hoping it was just jetlag, she turned to Mouse.

'Let's go see the cave I think Ebony should have.'

Mouse followed Joanna down the passage. To reach it they had to go round to the far side of the indoor arena. Joanna slid back the latch that kept the huge door shut, pushed the heavy wooden panels and went into the cave.

'What do you think? It's bit out of the way of the

other caves but it's got a high roof, some crevices for hiding, a smooth floor and good wing-beating space. I should say that this is the best and largest cave after Excelsior's. It also opens out into the arena, which is very handy for practising if the weather is bad. I expect Ebony will miss all that Californian sunshine.'

'Will you mind if Hannibal beats you on Ebony?' asked Mouse.

'Of course I'll mind!' exclaimed Joanna. 'Though not as much as XL. Why, do you think they will?'

Mouse looked at her friend in amazement. 'Er, *no*! I bet you continue to annihilate everyone.' Joanna nodded, only half convinced. 'Think I need to go and look at some of those headlines that said how brilliant I was . . .'

'Mouse get off OK?' asked Isaac the next morning. Joanna had bumped into him coming out of Vincent's study with an enormous book stuck under his arm.

'Yeah, she went off first thing,' sighed Joanna, already missing the way her friend livened everything up. 'I won't see her for ages now. Not until I go training in Wales. She's going to be staying with Giovanni and Lucia all August. I was invited too, but my mum's insisting we have a family holiday down in Cornwall visiting my cousins.'

'Cornwall and Wales, lucky you,' said Isaac. 'I'm

stuck in London all summer. Still I've got these to be getting on with.' He pointed to the book under his arm. 'This book's amazing. It's a history of the early dragon lords and the earliest races. And it's got some amazing pictures. Look.'

Isaac opened the book. Spread across the page was a great green dragon. Its belly was encrusted in fabulous rainbow coloured scales. Two vicious horns curved like scimitars crowned its long, triangular face. Underneath the dragon Joanna read the words, *Gemma dracone atrocissimus*. She didn't need to know much Latin to know what the words meant – *Jewel dragon, fiercest of all.* Joanna gave a shudder and quickly turned the page to see a man with a long black beard and a feathered red velvet hat, flying a rather fierce-looking silver dragon.'

'Do you think I should get a hat like that for the egg-turning?' asked Isaac.

Joanna wasn't sure if he was serious or not.

Later that morning Isaac paid a second visit to Vincent's study. He switched on a small desk light and sat in the armchair next to the fireplace. Its soft brown leather was beginning to wear a bit thin on the arms. Isaac liked to imagine Vincent sitting there thinking. He needed to think, too. Ever since his visit to the Devil's Slide Caves he'd been not just out of sorts, but troubled. He took a crumpled brochure out of his pocket. He'd read and reread it so many times. All the egg-turning at the Devil's Slide Caves was done by remote control. The turner's job seemed to consist of checking data and pressing a few buttons. But they obviously were getting results – Ebony was hatched by this process, her dragon parents having been genetically chosen for breeding a champion. They could turn and monitor any number of eggs. His head told him this was the future of egg-turning and yet his heart refused to believe that it could be true. Yet, if it was true, was it something he wanted to be part of? He would be taking his GCSEs next summer. Mr Hogan had already offered to tutor him for his A levels, saying that Isaac's academic needs couldn't be met in an ordinary sixth form. Alchemy wasn't exactly something you found on a school syllabus.

Isaac stood up and went over to the fireplace and touched the letters chiselled deep in the stone mantelpiece.

ignem amore accende

Light the fire with love. That wasn't data you could type into a computer. Neither could you measure how glad he'd been to see the egg again. It had grown much heavier whilst he'd been away. And the egg had grown darker in colour. They could keep their modern technologies. Egg-turning was far more than facts and numbers. Isaac smiled to himself. He was looking forward to discovering all the changes to the egg in the three months left before the dragon hatched. The egg's final turning was set for 7.30am on October the fourteenth and the dragon would hatch approximately six hours later. He knew he would be expected to conjure the Silver Flame, *spiritus draconis*, for the final turning of the dragon egg. Already he could imagine how the egg would look cradled in the silver fire.

He still wasn't sure how the fire worked, only that to make it he had to think about the things he cared most about. He closed his eyes, running his fingers over the carved indents in the stone. What did he love? In his mind's eye images of the golden egg came into view, followed by his grandma and family. Isaac gave a laugh – there was Excelsior breaking the world record and Joanna lifting the World Championship Cup. A small flicker of silver danced over his fingers . . .

His concentration was broken by the shrill ring of the telephone.

'Hello?'

He barely recognised the sound of his own voice as he answered the phone. It sounded as though it was coming from far away.

'Isaac?' It was Afra. 'I can't get Mike on his mobile so can you pass on a message for me? Ebony can't be moved for another week. The good news is Jamie's offered us a flight back with him on a special plane Heywood Consortium uses for transporting dragons.'

Isaac heard Afra break off for a second before he could answer. She came back on the phone.

'Oh and I have a message for you. Amber says hi!'

Isaac grinned. 'Tell her I say hi back.'

Spiky Mike just shrugged his shoulders at Isaac's message. Joanna thought he looked a bit miserable as he disappeared into his office. She turned back to Isaac looking rather dismayed.

'What's the matter?' asked Isaac.

'He's missing Afra of course,' said Joanna indignantly. 'And he doesn't like Jamie Penhaligon. I think he's an old boyfriend of Afra's.'

'So?'

'So he might try and . . .' Joanna saw the look on Isaac's face and her voice trailed away.

'Get real, Jo. Spiky Mike and Afra are rock solid.'

Joanna just nodded in agreement, embarrassed Isaac thought her suspicions ridiculous. But there was something about Jamie Penhaligon that she didn't trust. Didn't trust at all.

7
PREPARATIONS

From: Adam Braithwaite
To: admin@t&c_enterprises.com

Why the silence?
Have you located Jewel dragon?

From: admin@t&c_enterprises.com
To: Adam Braithwaite

Just finalising travel arrangements to UK.
Penhaligon is expecting you.
News of Jewel dragon expected soon.

From: Adam Braithwaite
To: admin@t&c_enterprises.com

Liar

A contact of mine will give you a call regarding the purchase of the Jewel dragon

Cash up front

Unmarked dollar bills

In the penthouse suite of an exclusive hotel in San Francisco a man was looking critically at his reflection in the bathroom mirror. Marius King hardly recognised himself anymore. The plastic surgery on his nose, making it longer and straighter, had been very successful. His hair was cut very short and dyed dark brown. He'd grown a moustache and beard and disguised his eyes behind a pair of tinted heavy rimmed glasses. He was thinner too, but he felt better for the lost pounds. His one regret was changing his smart designer suits in favour of a more casual look – light-coloured chinos, an open-necked shirt, and his one indulgence to himself – an expensive tan leather jacket. Was it a good enough disguise for his return to the UK? Certainly it had fooled Joanna Morris at the World Championships. How he'd laughed watching her get so upset at the WDRF official taking a test sample when he himself had been standing only a few metres away. He hoped she'd reacted similarly on finding her crushed flowers and his little 'note'. But such things were mere trifles, just to keep her on edge. They were nothing to what he had planned next. For the past five months he'd been busy weaving his web of under-the-radar connections, calling in favours, and making some very lucrative business deals. Now everything was ready. Why, he'd transferred one million dollars into an offshore account that very afternoon. He picked up his passport and looked at the name printed there.

Dr Adam Braithwaite

This time tomorrow he would be boarding a large exclusive yacht ready to set sail across the Atlantic Ocean. Just outside UK waters he'd rendezvous with 'friends', who would see him safely ashore, away from the prying eyes of the coastguard.

'Home. Soon I'll be home and then . . . and then I'll never be troubled by Joanna Morris or her dragon ever again.'

8
EBONY ARRIVES
IN BRIXTON

The morning Ebony was due to arrive at the Brixton Caves finally arrived. Not that Spiky Mike allowed Joanna and Excelsior any time off from their own training schedule and insisted Joanna take Excelsior out for his early morning flight as usual.

'Where do you fancy flying?' asked Excelsior as they prepared to fly. 'We could go over to Richmond Park, or how about flying to Greenwich? You know how you love seeing the Cutty Sark.'

'But they'll take too long and we might miss Ebony's arrival,' said Joanna. 'I was just thinking of a quick trip up to the park.'

As they flew up over Brixton towards the park Joanna couldn't help but notice how slowly Excelsior was flying. 'What's with the snail pace?' She prodded him in the mind-blend to go a bit faster.

'I'm enjoying the sunshine,' came his reply. 'What's the hurry to meet Ebony anyway?'

Joanna smiled. Was this an example of Excelsior asserting himself as the alpha dragon in the caves that Spiky Mike had told her about? She never associated Excelsior with all that macho stuff – perhaps she was wrong.

She decided to drop all further mention of Ebony and just enjoy the flight. Excelsior was right – it was a gorgeous summer morning. Down below in the park joggers chased after them as they slalomed through the trees and the early morning swimmers in the open-air Lido waved up in greeting. Flying over the playing field they came upon Joanna's old primary school getting ready to hold their annual sports race, so Excelsior decided to entertain them with a spectacular series of dives and loop the loops.

It was only as they turned back for the Brixton Caves that Excelsior decided to voice his niggles about Ebony.

'Of course I have no doubt as to my ability to beat her in a race, but I *am* pretty annoyed that she'll have spent the previous week scouring Hannibal's mind for all our tricks. . . and apparently she eats ground steak! What's wrong with a good bucket of chicken livers?'

They spent the rest of the flight trying to second-guess what their rivals were planning for the coming season, their guesses become wilder and more extravagant.

By the time they got back, Ebony had already arrived and was settling down in her cave. Spiky Mike suggested that Joanna wait to bring Excelsior down to meet Ebony until after lunch. He was obviously very pleased Afra was back, because he'd lost his grumpy look and was whistling as he walked out of the cave.

What shocked Joanna was bumping into Hannibal coming up the passage from Ebony's cave. Last time she had seen him his hair was in a soft Afro, now it was braided in tight, thin, straight cornrows. Gone were his baggy designer jeans, basketball shirt and trainers, instead he was dressed in an all black leather racing suit. He looked older, sharper, more like the rival he was. He nodded briefly to Joanna and walked past without speaking.

Dismayed and shocked, Joanna hurried back to Excelsior.

'Perhaps we can't be friends during a race, but he was just plain rude. That's not like him at all.'

At two o'clock Joanna and Excelsior made their way down to the indoor flight cave.

The arena was lit from above by floodlights. Along

one wall stood Spiky Mike, Joanna and Excelsior, and on the opposite side Afra, Hannibal and Ebony. Joanna felt like she was taking part in some strange dance. Who would make the first move?

Excelsior took the initiative. He flung his wings open wide and walked slowly towards Ebony. He was breathing fire and a haze of smoke trailed behind as he moved to the very centre of the cave.

He stopped, folded his wings carefully to his side and waited.

Slowly, very slowly, Ebony walked towards him, head held high. She was as beautiful as Joanna remembered. She shone silky black under the bright floodlights, neck curved like a swan's, and her silver eyes sparkling imperiously.

The others in the cave were little more than irrelevant bystanders in this meeting of the two dragons. What would they do if the dragons hated each other? Joanna desperately wanted to listen into their thoughts and wondered if Hannibal was thinking the same. He refused to look at her and kept his eyes firmly on Ebony.

The dragons circled each other warily, each holding each other's gaze, when suddenly Excelsior stopped dead in his tracks and gave a quick roar.

'Look Ebony,' he said so that everyone could hear. 'We don't need to play power games. You are welcome in these caves, but I'm world champion. It's up to you to beat me.'

Ebony looked rather taken aback, but not angry or annoyed. Instead she turned round and walked – rather elegantly, Joanna thought – back to Hannibal.

As the tension in the cave evaporated, Afra began to laugh.

'I thought for one minute there we were going to have the most terrible deadlock, with the dragons eyeballing each other for the rest of the day. Did you see them? I can't tell you how relieved I am it's all over.'

She was gabbling so fast, no one could understand her. It was so unlike her usually calm self that Spiky Mike looked quite alarmed.

'Come on let's get these dragons back in their caves, and then you need to go home to get some sleep. I, er, think you need it.'

Back in his cave Excelsior was (for him) very modest about the meeting.

'It wasn't a big deal really; I'm not sure what all the fuss is about.'

'What did you think of her?' asked Joanna. ' Do you think you'll get on OK? Did you like her?'

'You always ask me questions like that. It's not a question of like or not. She's a racing dragon. I want to beat her and she wants to beat me. We really are quite independent creatures you know. It's not like with you fancying Dominic or . . .'

Joanna glared at her dragon. 'I don't know what you're talking about. Isaac and I are just good friends.'

'Did I even mention Isaac's name?' was Excelsior's comment.

9
VISITORS

Hannibal announced his training plans the next morning. He was going to train down in Brighton at the Pavilion Caves. It was nothing personal against Joanna, but as she was his chief rival he preferred that they train separately. Afra needed to be in Brighton too, overseeing the plans for the new dragon flying school that she and Spiky Mike were opening the follow September.

Joanna had been very upset by the whole conversation, so she wasn't in the best of moods when Dominic rang to ask a favour. He'd delayed going to South Africa for a few days and was down in Cornwall buying the Penhaligon dragon. Would it be possible for Dr Penhaligon to drop the dragon off in Brixton next weekend as he would be in London and then his Nan's friend could pick it up to take it back to Suffolk?

Joanna was gobsmacked. Not even a *thank you for inviting me to the World Championship races* text from Dominic since they'd got back from the States and now he was phoning solely to ask her if the Brixton Caves could do him a favour – and Joanna was sure she could hear Amber giggling in the background.

Joanna waited a second before saying as coolly as she could, 'You'll have to ask Spiky Mike. I'm sure your nan must have his number. If not, perhaps Amber can help you find it.'

Somehow Dominic's nan must have persuaded Spiky Mike, because early the following Sunday morning Joanna and her trainer waited as Jamie Penhaligon arrived in a huge, state-of-the-art, WDRF dragon transporter. As he pulled the shiny red wagon into the loading bay, Joanna noticed that Jamie had a passenger. One flick of hair told her Amber had come along for the ride and Joanna watched with a sinking heart as Amber leapt down out of the passenger compartment and came over and air kissed them both. Joanna wasn't sure who was more horrified – her or Spiky Mike.

'Just had to come and see Brixton. I've heard *so* much about it and I've never met Excelsior. I mean to actually meet a World Champion is *so* exciting.' Amber was all smiles. 'Where is everyone?'

'Afra and Hannibal are down in Brighton getting a

cave ready for Ebony,' replied Joanna equally brightly. Two could play this game.

'And Isaac?'

'Somewhere around,' said Joanna, knowing full well he was down in the caves at that very moment feeding Ebony and Excelsior. 'He's always busy doing a trillion things in the caves.'

Why was Amber asking where Isaac was? *Please decide to do a long Latin translation with Mr Hogan*, Joanna willed Isaac.

Except there was Isaac coming up from the caves to stand alongside Spiky Mike.

'Hi Amber!' He stuffed his hands in his jeans pocket and smiled broadly. Joanna suddenly felt invisible. Had Isaac even noticed she was there?

'I told you I'd be able to persuade Jamie to bring me.' Amber beamed at Isaac, flicking her hair over her shoulder.

Joanna looked on stunned. Was Amber in contact with both Dominic *and* Isaac?

'Let me show you Lancelot,' said Amber taking Isaac by the arm and leading him around to the back of the transporter. Joanna followed them, feeling forgotten. The Scarlet Spiked-Back dragon was refusing to move and Spiky Mike and Jamie were discussing ways to get the dragon out, disagreeing with each other in the process.

'Why would you want to use an electric noose?' said Spiky Mike in an annoyed tone. 'Just try ordering him out in a simple mind-blend.'

'He's a feeling a bit nervous in new surroundings,' Amber whispered to Isaac. She turned to Spiky Mike. 'Shall I try and get the dragon out?'

Amber tottered up the ramp in her high-heeled boots and skinny jeans, flicking her hair as she went. Joanna found herself wanting to give it a good pull. How was she was appropriately dressed for delivering a dragon?!

Amber appeared to mind-blend with Lancelot, but still the dragon didn't move. Amber turned round and smiled apologetically. She tried again, but still the dragon wouldn't move.

'He's put up a mind-block.' she said finally.

'Never mind, Amber,' said Jamie. 'It was good to try. Now, let's prepare the electric noose.'

'Can I try?' Joanna climbed up the ramp as Amber took little teetering steps down. She walked up to the dragon's side. Just as Amber had said, the dragon had put up a mind-block to keep its thoughts private. Joanna prodded a little further. The dragon wasn't expecting that and dropped its defences. It seemed agitated and very nervous, so as gently as she could she spoke her thoughts to the dragon.

My name is JoJo; at least that's what my dragon calls

me. You are very welcome in our caves. Would you like to come down and see them now? You can choose which one you want to stay in, and then Isaac will prepare something really tasty for you to eat. How about chicken livers? That's my dragon's favourite.

What about the other one? asked Lancelot nervously.

What other one? said Joanna, rather perplexed at the question.

The one from America, replied Lancelot in a whisper.

Do you mean our new dragon, Ebony? asked Joanna, wondering if Amber had mentioned her. *She likes ground steak. You can have that if you prefer?*

The other dragon, I don't want to meet it, said Lancelot. Joanna noticed he was trembling. She gently placed her hand upon his back for a few seconds. It was enough for Lancelot to start making his way down the ramp

Joanna watched as Spiky Mike and Jamie led the dragon into the lift to take it down to the caves. What was all that about? Lancelot seemed fine now he was in the lift.

Amber smiled a sickly smile at Joanna and started to follow Isaac down the stairs when she pretended to trip.

'Oops! Didn't realise the steps would be quite so steep.'

Isaac's response, as Joanna and Amber both knew

it would be, was to offer his arm and tell Amber to hang on.

It was more than Joanna could bear.

'Let me through then,' she said and slipped lightly past and zipped down two at a time. Behind her she could hear Amber laughing with Isaac.

'If Amber comes in here, ignore her!' Joanna flung herself down by Excelsior's side.

'What, Amber the girl with the flicky hair you met in the States?' questioned Excelsior, 'What's she doing here?'

'She's all over Isaac, it's disgusting.' Joanna pulled a face. 'Apparently she's been contacting him – Facebooking him or texting or something.'

'I thought she was eyeing up Dominic,' said Excelsior.

'Looks like it's both of them!' exploded Joanna.

'Never mind, you've got me,' said Excelsior. 'What's Dominic's dragon like then?'

'He's called Lancelot and I really liked him . . . except he was really scared and wouldn't get out of the transporter van. He seemed bothered about Ebony, unless Jamie's got some other dragon in there. The van's enormous. I certainly didn't hear any other dragon though.

'Ooh!' exclaimed Excelsior enthusiastically,

'Perhaps there's a hidden compartment and Jamie's really a smuggler.'

'I was joking' replied Joanna disparagingly.

'All the same,' said Excelsior, 'it wouldn't hurt to take a quick look.'

'Dr Penhaligon won't be too happy if he finds me snooping round his van,' said Joanna.

She thought for a moment and then took out one of her earring studs.

'I'll pretend I dropped it in the van and just went to find it.'

Joanna hurried up the stairs to the loading area. The Brixton vans looked rather old-fashioned and shabby next to Jamie's juggernaut. She slipped between the vehicles and made her way round to the back of the huge van. The back door had been rolled down shut. Carefully and as quietly as she could she rolled up the door a fraction and slipped inside. Immediately she knew she wasn't alone. It was too dark to see, but she didn't need to see them to recognise Amber's giggles and to hear Isaac say, 'Who's there?'

Horrified she rolled quickly back out and ran back towards the stairs.

'Jo?' Isaac had rolled up the door and come after her.

She turned round to face him saying as naturally as she could, 'Sorry . . . I didn't know anyone was there

'. . . I dropped one of my earrings and I thought it might be in the transporter, so I came to look for it.'

Isaac turned to Amber, who was watching from the back of the transporter.

'Jo thinks she dropped an earring. Have you got a torch or anything in the front?'

Amber jumped down reluctantly and, after what seemed an age, returned with a large powerful torch, that she flashed directly into Joanna's eyes.

'This do?' she said, smiling at Isaac.

Isaac took the torch and jumped back into the cavernous interior. Holding it up high, he called back.

'Have a look now Jo.'

As Joanna started to search the floor Amber came up beside her, pretending to look too.

Joanna moved away, ignoring Amber. She turned to Isaac.

'Can you just shine it a bit closer over in that corner?'

Isaac walked over directing the beam of light, leaving Amber behind in the darkness. Joanna quickly bent down and pretended to pick up the earring she had been holding all along. She put her hand on the wall to steady herself and a flicker of angry dragon fire flashed through her mind. It happened so quickly that she wondered if she'd imagined it.

'Found my earring,' she cried quickly, hoping her

voice was trembling too much. 'I'm so glad I found it – it was a birthday present from Mouse.'

'What's going on here?' Jamie suddenly appeared in the doorway. He sounded cross. 'I told you not to mess around in here Amber.

'We were only looking for Joanna's earring,' said Amber. 'Stop making such a fuss.'

'I'm the one who'll be answerable to Cliff Heywood if anything happens to his dragon.'

'I thought you said it was sedated,' grumbled Amber.

'Have you got another dragon in the transporter then?' asked Joanna as innocently as she could.

Dr Penhaligon quickly confirmed he'd picked up a dragon earlier that morning to drive down to Tintagel. It was for a new research project headed by a Dr Adam Braithwaite. He turned back to his sister. 'And that means we need to be off.'

'Spoilsport,' muttered Amber. 'Just because Afra's not here.'

'That'll do Amber.' Her brother glared at his sister. 'Remember you're not supposed to be here at all.'

With a flick of her hair Amber flounced passed Joanna and climbed up in to the passenger cabin.

'I'll be in touch Isaac,' she called from the window, 'Glad you found your earring, Joanna,' she added a little too sweetly.

10
TINTAGEL

The heavy swell of sea pushed the boat softly into shallow water allowing its occupants to jump over the side and pull the boat up on to the sand. They dragged the boat clear of the water, feeling their way up the blackness of beach.

It was a dark night with only a wafer thin moon to illuminate their surroundings. One of the boatmen flashed a brief signal out to sea. Darkness returned to the beach, and it was hardly possible to see that someone had arisen from the boat. With the help of the two boatmen he climbed out of the boat and moved quickly across the sand and vanished into the night.

The boatmen dragged the boat back to the sea, disappearing as quickly as they had come. The whole incident had taken less than five minutes. It barely happened.

Marius King turned away from the sea and up the track that led to a waiting car. It was just a short journey along the cliff road to Penhaligon Manor. The car had barely pulled up before Marius was out and rapping firmly on the front door.

'Coming,' the sound of a man's voice called out from behind the closed door. Marius King waited impatiently, stamping his feet on the doormat, as he heard the sound of a bolt being slid out of place.

Marius held out his hand, a supercilious smile on his lips.

'Penhaligon?'

His host shook his hand vigorously.

'Dr Braithwaite, welcome to Tintagel Manor.'

Marius King awoke next morning to the smell of bacon and toast. A girl was chattering loudly on her phone outside his door. He looked at the clock on his bedside table. It was already nine o'clock. Time for Dr Braithwaite to join the Penhaligons.

Downstairs the family were breakfasting and bickering in equal amounts. Marius King waited outside the dining room for a few moments to hear their conversation. Family squabbles were such an invaluable source of information.

'Amber! I've told you before, you have to show the visitors around the caves.' snapped Julian Penhaligon.

'Only if you pay me.'

Marius recognised the voice of the girl he'd heard on the phone.

'You'll do as you're told, young lady, and help out.' insisted her father.'

'What, because you're too stingy to hire someone?' Amber shouted back.

Marius didn't hear Julian's reply, but its effect was immediate, for the next moment Amber Penhaligon stormed out of the room. Seconds later the front door slammed shut. He waited a few seconds and went into breakfast.

'My apologies for the rudeness of my daughter,' said Julian apologetically. 'During term time she lives with her mother up in London and pretty much does as she pleases.'

'Dad!' replied Jamie. 'That's a bit harsh.'

'See,' replied Julian, sipping his tea with a sigh. 'What chance do I have? Mother and brother spoil her. Why, only last week she snuck off to London without a by your leave to deliver a dragon with Jamie. All I got was a text message that I could barely understand. Now, if you'll excuse me, I must open up the caves. Jamie will look after you.'

Marius filled up his plate with scrambled egg, bacon, sausage and grilled tomato – this was to be his home for the foreseeable future and he was determined to enjoy his stay as much as possible.

'Your father finds your sister a bit of a handful?' suggested Marius, biting with relish into a hot sausage. Why did home-cooked food in the UK taste better than anywhere else?

'She's just young and bored. Dr Braithwaite. And she wants to race – even more so since she met our world champion.'

'Amber's met Joanna Morris?' asked Marius, trying not to show too much interest.

'A couple of times actually,' said Jamie. 'Although I think Amber's more interested in Joanna's friends, Dominic Pieterson and Isaac – that boy who works in the Brixton caves.'

'Isaac, isn't he the boy who saved the dragons from the flu virus?' A smile spread across Marius' face. He loved it when pieces just fell into place of their own accord.

'I must say these sausages are really delicious,' said Marius smiling at Jamie. 'I think I'll have another. Perhaps you can persuade your sister to give me a guided tour later . . . after the visitors have gone of course.'

Amber took off down to the beach, first making a detour to the kitchen to load up with supplies for the day. Her family had private access to a small cove that could be reached via the dragon caves and it was her favourite place to escape.

She lay down on her beach mat, in the shelter of the rocks. It was a perfect suntrap. Sunglasses, music on and hot, hot sun. She fingered the necklace around her neck; the piece of amber was already warm to touch. She held up the chain to admire the tiny insects trapped inside the resin. She remained undiscovered for the whole morning, but just as she was about to emerge from her hideout for a swim Amber heard a man's voice. Was that her dad come to find her? She hated showing people round the dragon caves. Worst of all, she had to wear a faux medieval dress and pretend to be an Arthurian heroine. But it wasn't her dad; it was the man who'd arrived suddenly yesterday evening. He was standing in the opening of the cave mouth. She could hear him talking to someone behind him, inside the cave, and she crept closer to listen. Dr Braithwaite was saying something about recovery time to injured dragons. Had to be Jamie he was talking to, then. So she was safe from her dad for a while longer.

Safely hidden behind the rocks, she was about to jam in her earphones to block out the man's voice when he said, ' . . . you're sure the early morning tide will clear all signs of the fight?'

Fight! Amber was burning with curiosity now.

'And everything will be in place by Friday night?' Amber could see the man through a crevice in the rocks. She scrambled closer in the hope of hearing her brother's reply, but he was too far back in the cave to be heard.

The visitor disappeared back into the cave and Amber stayed hidden in the rocks, going over everything she'd just heard. Her brother was helping organise some kind of fight on the beach. What sort of grisly research was their visitor involved in? It didn't seem like Jamie's cup of tea at all, yet she knew he was desperate to make a name for himself in the dragon world. Was this why he'd been so on edge since they'd got back from the States? She'd put his irritability down to the fact he'd discovered Afra was engaged to Joanna's bad-tempered trainer. Amber jumped up out of her hiding place and ran into the sea. She was scared and excited all at the same time. Should she tell her brother that she knew or keep it a secret?

II
A CORNISH
HOLIDAY

The second week of the holiday with her Cornish cousins was drawing to a close. The glorious sunny weather meant Joanna had her wish of sunbathing and swimming. She was more than content to listen to George's band practising and spend time painting in a small wood at the back of the house with Lucy, who was the same age as Jo. At present she was designing a T-shirt for the band, The Acorns, to sell at their gigs.

Joanna was helping, rubbing a gold wax crayon rather frantically across the paper she had flattened to a tree – Lucy wanted to put together lots of different textures in her design. 'Put together' was a very good way to describe Jo's cousin, who wore a collection of clothes from various second-hand market stalls and charity shops that she decorated with brooches and embroidery and safety pins.

'Is that what you want to do then, be a designer?' asked Joanna. She hadn't done anything like this since the infants and was rather enjoying watching the ripples of wood appear on the paper.

'I'm not sure yet. After my A levels I'm going to apply to art school. How about you? Will you keep racing?'

'When I'm eighteen I'll be the legal owner of the Brixton Caves.'

'But what about uni and studying?'

Joanna didn't really know what to say. She hadn't thought about doing anything else before, but did she really want to keep winning the same races over and over again? And what about Excelsior? As he got older he would slow down and would he want to race if he didn't win . . . ? Would *she* want to race if he didn't? She followed her cousin slowly back to the house. Any further thoughts about her future were soon forgotten as her aunt came out to call them in.

'Good news, I've managed to get an extra day's holiday so I can take you to visit the Tintagel Dragon Caves tomorrow.'

It seemed that even when she was on holiday, Joanna couldn't escape the Penhaligons!

Joanna took a great deal of time dressing the next morning. She changed outfits three times. Each time she looked in the mirror she imagined Amber's face staring out at her. In the end she tossed on a pair of jeans and a T-shirt.

'You are not going to get to me,' she hissed at the mirror, much to her cousin's amazement.

It was only a quick journey up the coast to Tintagel and soon Joanna was queuing with a dozen other visitors for the eleven o'clock tour. From the ticket office Joanna could see over the top of a high brick wall to a large old house. She wondered which was Amber's room. The chances of them meeting were very small. She couldn't imagine Amber wanting anything to do with holiday makers. Just then the tour guide called everyone to attention. Everyone crowded round and Joanna found herself at the back. It was only as the guide started her welcome speech that Joanna wanted to get a closer look. She recognised that voice. She edged her way to the front just as the guide invited everyone to 'Follow in the footsteps of King Arthur, son of Uther Pendragon, who, legend tells us, was born in the castle nearby'.

Joanna couldn't believe her eyes! Instead of her usual designer jeans, there was Amber in some sort of medieval fancy dress. She was wearing a green velvet dress with a long golden belt and even a small gold crown. She still looked amazing, but at least her hair was plaited so there was no chance of any flicks!

Amber – tour leader? Joanna suspected Amber had not volunteered for the job.

It was obvious that Amber was equally surprised to see Joanna. Thrown off her stride, she stopped for a moment and stared. Then just as suddenly she blanked her and turned to the waiting visitors with a dazzling smile.

'Let's make our way into the caves.'

Joanna was happy to be ignored and followed at the back as everyone was led down steps cut into the rock. They made their way through a series of twisting tunnels until they came to a stop just outside a large cave.

Amber looked around at the expectant faces.

'The moment you have all been waiting for. You are about to enter a dragon's cave!'

A couple of young boys who had been shadowing Amber gave a quiet 'Yes!' Joanna smiled to herself, remembering the very first time she had gone into Excelsior's cave.

'This is the cave of the dragon Galahad, named after one of the Knights of the Round Table. He's a Scarlet Spiked-Back dragon. His younger brother, Lancelot, will be racing next season with the flyer Dominic Pieterson, who lost his own dragon so tragically in the recent influenza outbreak.'

Just as Amber had planned the visitors looked both impressed and sympathetic.

'He's a personal friend of mine,' continued Amber, casting a quick glance over in Joanna's direction, 'and I look forward to watching him race this coming season.'

And before anyone could make any further comments Amber swept ahead of the party into the cave, announcing as she went, 'On no account should you touch or feed the dragon.'

It was very 'Hollywood', with lights casting shadows on the high roof of the cave. There was also a substantial amount of dry ice wafting around so that Galahad loomed out of mist and shadows.

'Very dramatic and atmospheric,' whispered Joanna to her aunt, hoping it would please her. Her aunt, however, was somewhat distracted by the dragon breathing out a huge blast of fire at the roof of the cave. The two young boys were obviously impressed and started to roar and pretend to breathe fire back at Galahad.

Amber came rushing over.

'Get back! Stand away from the dragon.'

She turned to the dragon.

'Galahad, calm down!' But the dragon continued blasting the roof of the cave with a torrent of fire.

Joanna watched Amber's attempts at controlling Galahad with growing concern. The dragon was becoming more and distraught and Amber didn't seem to have a clue what to do. It began to dawn on the assembled party that this was not part of the tour. People were shuffling slowly backwards.

'Something has distressed Galahad so it's necessary we exit the cave immediately.' Looking rather flustered, Amber announced it was time to leave.

Joanna was following everyone out of the cave when she felt a sudden stab of pain and saw a huge twist of angry red flame flash behind her eyes. Behind her the dragon was now crouching low on the ground, cowering in fear. Joanna staggered against the wall as another flash of fire blazed through her mind. Then just as suddenly the fire slowly faded away into nothing. Still unable to walk Joanna stood leaning against the wall when suddenly Amber was standing beside her.

'I said get out of the cave! Just because you're world champion doesn't give you the right to ignore me. I'm responsible for your safety—'

'I'm feeling a bit faint,' said Joanna. 'Can you just get my aunt?'

'What? Again! Well you've got to wait in the passage,' said Amber.

'Amber, I can't move. Just get her,' insisted Joanna.

Luckily her aunt returned at that moment to find Joanna. Instantly Amber was all concern.

'Joanna's feeling faint.'

Joanna had to be helped out of the cave by leaning on her aunt.

'I'll go and get some help,' said Amber, disappearing down the passage.

'I heard you fainted in San Francisco too,' said her aunt, very concerned. 'I think your mother should get your blood pressure checked.'

'No, Aunty Margaret, it's not that. It's when something's wrong with a dragon and I pick up the emotion. You don't understand.'

'So what was wrong with him?' asked her aunt, looking back at Galahad's cave.

'He was frightened,' said Joanna, still feeling weak.

'Probably got upset by those young boys roaring at it. They were rather over excited,' commented her aunt.

Joanna nodded. Let Aunty Margaret think that. What she hadn't told her was it wasn't Galahad that had caused her such anguish. Just like Joanna, he'd been reacting – to another dragon.

When ten minutes had passed and Amber still hadn't returned, her aunt began to get annoyed.

'That girl's obviously forgotten all about us. Are you feeling well enough to walk now, Joanna?'

Joanna was happy to follow her aunt up the passage. They were fine until they came to a junction of three tunnels. Her aunt sighed in exasperation.

'You would think there would be signs telling you which way to go.'

'Aunty Margaret, just wait,' said Joanna. 'I'm sure Amber will be back in a minute.'

'Look there's a door just down there, marked private. I'm going to knock.'

Joanna's aunt disregarded her niece's protests and knocked loudly on the door.

A few seconds later they heard a man's voice call out, 'Who's there?'

Joanna's aunt opened the door.

'I'm sorry to disturb you, but my niece . . .'

Standing just behind her aunt, Joanna caught sight of Jamie Penhaligon crouching down. Next to him was a dragon, lying unconscious on the cave floor and clearly sedated. The dragon was mostly hidden in shadow, but Joanna could see that its claws were exceptionally long and razor-sharp. In an instant Jamie was outside the cave and closing the door. He was looking quite annoyed.

'Sorry guys, but this part of Tintagel Caves is private, didn't you see the notice?'

Joanna's aunt wasn't intimidated by Jamie at all.

'My niece was taken ill in one of your caves. We have been waiting for *ten minutes* for help.'

Jamie suddenly recognised Joanna but before he could say anything, Julian Penhaligon appeared hurrying down the passage.

'I'll deal with this, Jamie.'

Joanna watched Jamie disappear back through the door marked private. She was pretty sure the unconscious dragon was the one causing all the trouble. It had to be the one from the transporter. But why did it always have to be sedated?

'Here she is! Nothing to worry about!' said Julian Penhaligon to the waiting tour group at the exit to the caves. 'Our world champion is safe and sound.'

Joanna gave everyone a quick wave. Did Julian Penhaligon *have* to say she was world champion? She'd been rather relieved to have gone unrecognised so far.

'We wondered if it was you!' The mother of the two young boys came forward. 'Would you mind if we took a photo? That's if you're feeling better now.'

Amber slammed the door to her room behind her and ripped off the long green velvet dress.

'I am never, *ever* doing that again!' She grabbed her best designer jeans and favourite shirt and flung them on. That Joanna Morris, of all people, should have seen her dressed up so ridiculously! She vigorously brushed out her braided hair. And what was up with Galahad! Amber suspected that Joanna had done some strange mind-blend and got him to react like that so that she could do her fainting act again. It was pathetic.

She had to keep out of her dad's way. He'd be expecting her for the afternoon tour. She didn't even have Jamie on her side these days. When she mentioned she knew all about his new project, he'd snapped back her, saying she hadn't the faintest idea what he did for work and that it was about time she did something to help about the place herself.

She crept silently down the stairs and had nearly made it out of the front door, when she heard her dad's voice behind her.

'Not so fast, young lady. If you won't help, then you can spend the rest of the day up in your room.'

He actually frogmarched her back up the stairs.

Amber had never felt so angry in her life. How dare her treat her like some kid? She refused to stay in her room. She waited until she knew he would be busy with the afternoon tour and went down to the beach. To get there she had to go through the caves, but she timed it perfectly, tagging on to the end of the tour group before slipping away down to the beach.

12
FIGHT
CLUB

It was already late when the sun finally deserted the sky, leaving an inky blackness to descend over the small empty cove. Finally, just before midnight, a crowd of shadowy figures emerged out of the Tintagel caves to take their place on the sandy beach, marked off by a simple rope. Voices were low and hushed; faces hidden, fearful of recognition. A few brave watchers came forward and stood as close to the rope as they dared, eager for the action to begin. Slowly the nervous tension of the crowd began to grow. Excited breath caught in throats, cries escaped, heartbeats raced. When would the fight begin? Halfway up the cliff behind them, two bright floodlights powered on, revealing a flat sandy arena left behind by the retreating sea that was hurrying out of the cove. But all eyes were fixed on the cave entrance as two metal cages rumbled out on to the sand.

A voice over a loud speaker announced the contenders. First was Geronimo, a sturdy Rocky Mountain dragon imported from the USA. A veteran fighter, his battle scars were plain for all to see. The deep crimson red dragon beat his head against the metal bars, eager to escape his confines. His opponent was a Sumatran Blue, another male that went by the name of Krakatoa. He was a longer and leaner dragon and this was his first fight. Already a torrent of fire was pouring from his opened mouth and all along his back the spikes were flexed in aggression.

A single bell rang out and the doors were released.

A blood-curdling roar exploded from the watchers as the dragons flung themselves into the arena. Enraged by the very presence of a rival they began to circle each other.

Everyone waited spellbound, watching to see who would make the first move . . . and then, before anyone realised, the Sumatran Blue pounced on to Geronimo's back, raking his razor sharp talons across his wings. The red dragon roared in pain but, using its back legs as a lever, flung Krakatoa off. The watching spectators roared in approval as Krakatoa landed awkwardly, allowing Geronimo to fling its superior weight down with a crash, but the blue dragon was too fast and rolled expertly out of reach. Once more the two creatures started to slowly circle each other. The second attack came suddenly with a blast of fire as Krakatoa hurled his spikes towards Geronimo's underbelly. But the red dragon was expecting the move and, with perfect timing, turned side on. The spikes smashed against the red dragon's flank, but were unable to penetrate the larger, tougher side scales. The Sumatran Blue hesitated for a moment then launched in to the air ready for a second attack. Geronimo attempted to follow him into the air, but as he spread open his wings the damage from talon raking became obvious to all. He could barely fly. Geronimo was crouching low on the ground as his opponent came hurtling straight towards him, sensing victory. With a final effort the red dragon reared up on to his hind legs and launched himself forward whilst tearing at Krakatoa's head and neck with his outstretched talons. The Sumatran Blue breathed a rage of fire and smoke and tried to slither passed him, but Geronimo was already hurling all his weight violently down on top of Krakatoa. The blue dragon slid helpless to the ground. Geronimo pounded Krakatoa in a relentless fury until the blue dragon lay like a limp rag, his neck bent at a strange angle. Standing triumphantly over his victim, Geronimo arched his neck and blasted the air with a stream of fire. Krakatoa's only response was a twitching head and an occasional spasm that ran through his body. Victory to Geronimo! A bell rang out announcing that the fight was over. The spectators stood there reluctant to move; barely able to believe the spectacle they had witnessed had ended. Unaware that they too were being watched . . .

Nobody saw the girl hiding behind the rocks, fearful and fascinated by the bloody death of a dragon trampled mercilessly underfoot. They couldn't know that their secret was out nor what the young witness would decide to do . . .

13
MEET THE
DRAGONETTES

Despite the fine weather breaking half way up the motorway, deluging everything in a heavy summer downpour, Joanna was really looking forward to her visit to the Balivos' Dragon Sanctuary in North Wales. Her family had no idea how much she'd missed Excelsior, but there was no way of explaining it to someone who had never experienced a mind-blend and the immediacy of feeling a dragon's thoughts. How Excelsior was always aware of the direction of the wind, or his bliss as he slowly glided high in a cloudless sky or his crazy excitement as he spun the fire in his belly until he was almost giddy. How he knew how she was feeling without having to say a word.

Giovanni had picked her up at the service station near Bristol after collecting a delivery for the dragon sanctuary.

'Just wait until you see what I'm carrying in the back of the transporter van,' said Giovanni with a twinkle in his eye. 'I'm depending on you to keep them all quiet. Jabbering away they've been for hours, driving me nuts! Even Mouse would have trouble keeping up with them.'

Joanna was intrigued, but Giovanni wouldn't tell her what 'they' were.

'You'll find out soon enough,' he laughed.

Despite what Giovanni had told her, it all seemed very quiet in the back of the van. She sat very still and listened . . . silence. She looked across at Giovanni questioningly. He just buckled up his seat belt.

'Three!' He turned the key in the ignition. 'Two.' The van roared into life and pulled out of the car park. 'One!' he sighed. 'Bingo!'

Squeals and unintelligible chattering could be heard coming from the back of the van. Joanna quickly slid back the grill to the back of the van and peered at the large cage. Inside she could see three identical bright turquoise miniature dragons. Then, before her eyes, their scales shimmered and turned emerald green, before slipping suddenly into bright gold. Joanna turned back to Giovanni.

'Who are they? They're amazing! How do they change colour like that?'

'They're Chameleon dragons – very rare. I'm

babysitting them for a week before they're needed for a film at Pinewood Studios.'

'Film-star dragons?' exclaimed Joanna. 'XL will love that!'

'They're collectively known as the Dragonettes.' said Giovanni. 'But I'll let them tell you their own names.'

'Dragonettes! Brilliant!' Joanna thought for a moment. 'I think I'll communicate in a nice light breezy mind-blend.'

Giovanni laughed loudly. 'I'm leaving everything in your capable hands.'

Joanna sat back in her seat to concentrate on asking the questions that would take her into a mind-blend.

'What are you?' she asked.

Three voices replied in unison. 'We are the Dragonettes, stars of stage and screen! Calliope! Melpomene! Terpsichore! Triplets born from one egg!'

'And who?' (Calliope)

'May we ask?'(Melpomene)

'Are you?' (Terpsichore)

'I'm Joanna Morris, otherwise known as JoJo,' replied Joanna, trying hard not to laugh too much.

'What? The World Champion!' (Calliope)

'Who flies Excelsior?' (Melpomene)

'The Silver Spiked-Back dragon!' (Terpsichore)

'OOOHHH!' they chorused. 'We're such fans!'

All three Dragonettes spoke at once, in high voices, at full volume and top speed, all declaring undying love for Excelsior and could Joanna PLEASE arrange an introduction . . .

By now Joanna was crying with laughter. 'I'll see what can be arranged! But, if you are to meet Excelsior, shouldn't you get as much beauty sleep as possible?'

'Beauty sleep?' (Calliope)

'Of course!' (Melpomene)

'My eyes are shut already!' (Terpsichore)

And with that all three Dragonettes fell silent.

'Not sure what XL'll make of them,' said Joanna. 'How is he? I've missed him so much.'

'Missing you too,' smiled Giovanni. 'He hasn't been able to keep still for the last couple of days. When I left yesterday he was tearing up and down the mountainside at breakneck speed.'

Joanna smiled. She was looking forward to some mountain flights herself.

They drove on in silence until Giovanni said, 'I was disappointed Hannibal chose not to train Ebony in Wales. I was looking forward to a few races.'

Joanna pursed her lips. 'You're not the only one. Before they left for Brighton Hannibal and I had words. He said he needed to be my rival, not my friend, if he was going to beat me. D'you think he's right?'

'It's always a tricky one that,' said Giovanni thoughtfully. 'I don't think Spiky Mike and Afra will mind me telling you they've had to struggle with the same problem themselves. I wouldn't take it personally.'

'And poor Mouse – her chance to corner Hannibal on the mountainside gone once again,' said Joanna.

'Oh I think you'll find Mouse surviving well enough,' said Giovanni with a grin. 'Did I tell you we've got Lucia's nephew staying with us this summer?'

The weather brightened up and Giovanni made good time so that just before five o'clock they turned into the long driveway – past the gateway entrance with its two stone dragons standing guard – that led to the Snowdonia Dragon Sanctuary. Joanna waited for her first glimpse of the large, grey pebble-dashed house, surrounded by blue hydrangeas and golden gorse bushes. Behind the house the mountain soared, stern and majestic up to a blue cloudless sky.

Suddenly there was Mouse running out of the front door. She was waving and calling to Joanna, followed by a boy with dark curly hair and then, behind him, Lucia. Even though he was twice her height there was no doubting the boy was Lucia's nephew. Joanna hopped down out of the van only to find herself accosted on both cheeks with two great smacks of red lipstick kiss from Lucia.

'Joanna! Growing again – you are taller than me now. Wonderful flying in America. See if you can teach Salvatore how it's done. He's come over from Naples to learn English and how to fly a dragon. He is terrible! At both!'

'Hi, Salvatore,' smiled Joanna broadly. Mouse was dancing around behind him, hands on her heart and rolling her eyes up at the sky. Salvatore's lack of English was of little concern to her!

Giovanni announced he was going to take the Dragonettes up to their cave.

He called to Joanna. 'Tea or dragon?'

'Dragon!' replied Joanna, climbing up into the van again. 'Sorry, Lucia, but I haven't see Excelsior for so long.'

'And Salvatore and I are dying to meet the Dragonettes,' said Mouse grabbing Salvatore by the hand and pushing him up into the van so that he was squashed in between the two girls.

Joanna allowed Mouse to do all the talking and sat there quietly as they drove up to the caves. She was going to see her dragon again. Her heart gave a little quiver. Arriving at the caves, she left the others to deal with the Dragonettes, now wide awake and chatting ten to the dozen and made her way to the cave deep within the mountain where she knew Excelsior was waiting.

There he was – shiny and silvery and fiery. She ran the last bit, and flung her arms around him. He felt warm and smooth and familiar. She could smell the smoky bonfire of his breath and sense the buzz of his thoughts. Joanna let out a deep sigh. It was more like coming home than anything she knew. For the first time in weeks she felt complete.

'So summer wasn't quite so hot without me was it?' boasted Excelsior. 'Anything interesting to tell me?'

Joanna was just going to tell Excelsior how she'd nearly fainted again when Excelsior started shaking his head from side to side and blinking his eyes. It seemed the Dragonettes were making their presence felt.

'They're stars of the silver screen,' smiled Joanna. 'And desperate to meet you . . .'

Excelsior looked horrified.

'Or shall we go and fly?'

They left the din of the caves, with Giovanni shouting instructions to keep the Dragonettes' cage shut until he gave the word, and escaped into the silence of the sky. Excelsior knew where all the best thermal air currents were to be found and soon they were gliding high above the mountain.

'Fancy speeding up?' suggested Joanna. Excelsior blasted out a great stream of fire and pounded the air with his wings. Joanna felt the surge of speed and let out a yell of her own that echoed off the mountainside. Soon the earth below vanished and she was aware only of the blueness of sky, the soft caress of the breeze and the long still silence. Why would she ever want to do anything else but fly?

But the peace and beauty of the afternoon flight was soon forgotten – the Dragonettes saw to that. Just before dawn the household was awoken by a series of explosions coming from the caves. A bleary-eyed Giovanni staggered down the stairs and out of the house, only to be followed immediately by Joanna and Mouse hastily putting fleeces over their pyjamas.

'Stay here!' insisted Giovanni as he started up a small motorbike that he kept for emergencies. 'I'll be quicker on my own and I don't know how safe it is.'

Of course the girls ignored him and ran up the path after him, soon joined by Salvatore, who'd been ordered by Lucia to bring them back. Knowing such a request would be ignored, he didn't bother to say anything. All three staggered up in the dark, talking worriedly as they went.

At the entrance of the caves Joanna started sending out thoughts to Excelsior. If the others could have seen her face in the dark they would have suddenly seen her mouth drop open. Instead all they heard was hysterical laughter.

'What is it?' asked Mouse. 'Jo! Stop laughing. What's happened?'

'It's the Dragonettes!' Joanna managed to say. 'Come on, I really want to see this. Poor Excelsior!'

They met Giovanni carrying one of the Dragonettes by the scruff of its neck. A silver tasselled cloak was caught on one of its claws – which was very possibly varnished in glittery gold nail polish – and trailing along the floor. The dragon was wailing in a high-pitched squeal

'Oh XL! I love you!!!'

Giovanni grimaced at the flailing dragon.

'I must have been out of my mind agreeing to look after them. I've already caught the other two and put them in one of the secured caves. Can you guys take care of your dragons?'

Joanna found Excelsior lying in the middle of the floor hidden under a pile of swirling diaphanous fabrics that shimmered and glimmered in the half-light of the safety lamps.

'BOO!'

He jumped up, throwing off a sequinned sheet only to reveal a face shimmering in green and gold glitter. His eyes were lined in black kohl and he'd been liberally sprayed with a flowery perfume. His claws matched the sparkly gold of the Dragonettes'. His spikes were woven and tied with a myriad of rainbow coloured ribbons and silken flowers.

'Giovanni stopped the party!' complained Excelsior indignantly. 'We've been having such fun. I think I look quite amazing! The Dragonettes are going to talk to the director to see if I can have a cameo in their next film . . .'

'There were explosions!' interrupted Joanna. 'We thought the caves were under attack.'

Excelsior suddenly looked guilty.

'Ah, that's because I thought I *was* under attack. The Dragonettes can do this thing with their fire that affects your emotions. By changing the colour of their fire they can make you laugh or cry, be angry or scared. They do it all the time in their films.'

'What do you mean?' asked Joanna astounded.

Excelsior's eyes sparkled with excitement. 'If they are in a tragic scene, they make their flame take on a bluish tinge and anyone nearby becomes extra sad. Amazing isn't it? I want to see if I can do it. Shall I try it on you?'

'No!' Joanna was horrified, 'I don't want you to be *making* me feel anything.'

But Excelsior wouldn't be stopped and he let out a flame tinged in pale pink.

A wave of happiness washed over Joanna.

Everything around her looked so beautiful, including the young man standing in the doorway. He had the most gorgeous curly black hair.

'Are you OK?' he asked full of concern.

Joanna gave a soft sigh, ran up to him, draped her arms around his neck and, standing on tip-toe, kissed him full on the lips! She stepped back and looked up at his face. Salvatore was standing in front of her, looking surprised, but not unhappy.

At the same moment Mouse appeared behind him staring in astonishment and horror. Embarrassed and somewhat bewildered, Joanna let go of the bemused Salvatore.

'Whoops!' called Excelsior mischievously. 'Looks like it really does work!'

Joanna turned quickly to Mouse.

'It wasn't me; it was Excelsior! The Dragonettes have taught him a trick.'

'I like this trick,' smiled Salvatore. 'Bravo XL, you do trick again?'

'NO!' cried Joanna.

'What's going on in here?' Giovanni appeared in the doorway.

'Joanna kissed Salvatore. Apparently it was some sort of trick . . .' said Mouse, somewhat tartly.

'Excelsior made this pink fire,' insisted Joanna. Surely Mouse didn't believe she'd done it on purpose?

104

'Pink Fire?' Giovanni smiled knowingly. 'I should perhaps have warned you. Mood Management – it's their speciality!' He turned to Excelsior. 'So the Dragonettes taught you how to do it? I don't suppose they told you there are side effects . . .'

'Like what?' Joanna ran across to Excelsior.

'Try and mind-blend,' said Giovanni.

Joanna leant against Excelsior. Immediately she pulled away, screwing up her face.

'That's horrible; it's like a high pitch whine.'

'It's because the brain connections are being deliberately scrambled and everything is bouncing merrily around, so you get feedback – a bit like you get with a microphone. A good night's rest will put it right soon enough,' replied Giovanni reassuringly. 'But in future I'd leave such party tricks to the Dragonettes.'

Between them they quickly cleaned up Excelsior, wiped off his eyeliner and nail polish and untangled the ribbons and fabrics.

'I like you best plain and simple,' whispered Joanna to Excelsior before they left him to sleep.

Unfortunately, Salvatore kept trying to slip his arm around Joanna on the way back. He obviously hadn't understood about the mood management! Then, much to Joanna and Mouse's annoyance, he blew Joanna a kiss before disappearing up the stairs.

'Sorry Mouse!' Joanna looked so apologetic that Mouse had to laugh.

In their bedroom, as she turned off the light, Mouse said, 'I might just ask the Dragonettes to make that pink fire for me . . . shame Hannibal isn't here.' She gave a yawn. 'Just one thing – was it nice?'

Joanna blushed bright red and wouldn't answer, relieved that Mouse couldn't see her face in the dark. She closed her eyes and pretended she'd fallen asleep to deter any further questioning. But she was very much awake. What she hadn't told *anyone* was that she thought she'd been kissing someone else. And that the person she had thought she was kissing was . . . Isaac!

14
A TRIP TO
THE BEACH

The week sped by with no further dramatic events and the weather was glorious, just clear blue skies and golden sun. By the time it got to Saturday it was almost too hot, so Joanna, Mouse and Salvatore flew to the top of the mountain in search of a breeze.

'I hate this heat,' said Joanna, staring out over the land to the sea. 'I feel all prickly, like something's going to burst. If it's still this hot tomorrow let's ask Giovanni if we can take the dragons to the beach. We can find a nice deserted bay, have a picnic and a swim and then fly over the sea!'

'Sounds excellent. I can show you this new acrobatic trick Ariadne and I do over the sea.' said Mouse as she stretched out to sunbathe on a warm flat rock. 'That's if I can move from here.'

'I'm going for another fly,' said Joanna, noticing that Salvatore had sat down next to Mouse.

She certainly didn't want to play gooseberry. Excelsior wasn't in the mood to fly fast, so they glided slowly round the mountain

It was only about ten minutes later when Joanna saw Mouse and Salvatore flying towards her.

'Nia says a huge storm's coming in fast over the sea.' Mouse called over to her friend. 'We need to find find shelter. Salvatore can't fly fast enough to get down before the storm breaks.'

Joanna looked over to where Salvatore was clinging desperately to Nia. The red welsh dragon gestured to Joanna to lead the way to Ariadne's old cave, nearby, The cave was only ever used when a dragon had to be kept in isolation, and would be empty.

They made it just in time as the first spots of heavy rain hit the dry ground.

It was a splendid storm to watch from inside the cave. The mountain seemed to swell in size as the dark storm clouds massed around the summit like a rumbling great ogre. Silver flashes of lightning outlined the lower crags making them look like ancient crones.

'It's like something out of *Lord of the Rings*!' gasped Mouse.' She turned to smile at Salvatore, but he was hiding at the very back of the cave.

The storm was over as quickly as it came and left behind it a fresh and wonderful day.

'I can't wait till tomorrow, I can hear the beach calling now!' said Joanna. 'Let's fly back down and ask Giovanni if we can go for a picnic.'

Joanna was in the kitchen buttering bread for sandwiches when Salvatore came running in.

'*Terpischore è scomparsa!*' he panted, out of breath. '*È volata via!* Flown away! Gone! I tell Lucia! Giovanni call you.'

Just then Lucia appeared at the door with a huge bag of apples. Joanna left Salvatore explaining everything in Italian in much greater detail.

'Mouse,' she called up the stairs to where her friend was busy packing up their swimming things. 'Come quick!'

Mouse leapt down the stairs two at a time.

'What's up?'

'Terpsichore has vanished. Come on, we need to help find her.'

Giovanni was looking more frazzled than Joanna had ever seen him. 'I should have guessed one of them would try something like this!'

'You mean she did it on purpose? Wasn't she frightened by the storm?'

Giovanni scoffed loudly.

'Frightened? I wish! Apparently she had some big bust up with the other two Dragonettes about wanting a solo career. I reckon she's trying to whip up some publicity. I can see the headline now – *Storm tossed dragon*.

He paced up and down the cave anxiously.

'Trouble is the Chameleon is not a very robust breed – they catch chills easily. We need to find her fast, so it's all hands on deck. Jo, if you take between here and the coast, Mouse and Salvatore can search the mountain and I'll do the countryside on the far side of the mountain. But if you haven't found her by three o'clock then come back here.'

Joanna and Excelsior were soon flying over a patchwork of green grass fields and the soft yellow of haystack-dotted stubble, all crisscrossed with dark hedges and grey, dry-stoned walls. Beyond lay a blue ribbon of sea, stretched out along the coast. The sky was clear and a brisk fresh breeze was blowing in from the sea, yet there was neither sight nor sound of the Dragonette. As they flew Joanna and Excelsior were listening intently, trying hard to catch a squeak or squeal.

They both heard it at the same time – a piercing, high-pitched wail that made the hairs on the back of

Joanna's neck stand on end. It was coming from the direction of the sea.

'Terpsichore!' cried Joanna. They were too far from the mountain to send any sort of message to Giovanni. They were on their own.

'Call to her, XL, tell her we're on our way.'

But even though Excelsior called out to the dragon so that she couldn't fail to hear him, Terpsichore couldn't or wouldn't acknowledge him.

They flew over a headland and below them, in a sandy cove, they saw what had caused Terpsichore to scream out in such terror. On the edge of the shore, tossed carelessly by the waves, was the rotting carcass of a dragon. Its blue skin was turning grey and hanging off its body in great hunks; the skull crushed and what was left of its wings were little more than shredded rags. High in the sky above, girl and dragon lurched unsteadily forward.

They caught sight of the Dragonette, halfway up the cliff, hiding in a gorse bush. But on seeing them approach Terpsichore panicked. She leapt out of the gorse, missed her footing and tumbled down to the sand below. The dragon wasn't moving, but Joanna could still hear her whimpers.

For a brief second Joanna and Excelsior hovered in the air, before swooping down to land on the sand just a few feet away from the shoreline. The sweet stench of rotting flesh overwhelmed Joanna and made her gag. Excelsior heaved and began to foam at the mouth. For a moment neither of them could move, and then slowly – very slowly – Excelsior started to crawl across the sand to where the limp body of Terpsichore lay.

With a surge of effort he tensed his shoulders and threw back his head, before breathing out a blanket of silver flame over the Dragonette. Instantly Terpsichore revived. She scrambled to her feet, never once taking her eyes off Excelsior. He breathed over her again and she unfurled her now deep turquoise wings and flew up into the air. Without looking back she disappeared back up over the headland.

'I told her to get back to her cave, or she'd have me to answer to,' said Excelsior grimly. His back was still turned away from Joanna.

'Let's get going ourselves, XL – it's disgusting. We need to tell Giovanni . . .'

But Excelsior didn't move. He wasn't listening. All his attention was concentrated on the dead dragon. He held his own body taut and alert, the silver spikes along his back flexed upright and his tail curved over his spine, like a giant scorpion's sting ready to attack.

'XL!' Joanna insisted, feeling increasingly frightened. 'Come away. It's dead!'

Excelsior slowly turned his head towards Joanna.

'I know, JoJo – so why do I feel so afraid?'

Joanna looked back at the monstrous bloated body as the rising tide shifted the carcass over, revealing its broken, twisted hind legs and long razor-sharp claws . . . claws that Joanna had seen only a week ago in the Penhaligons' Tintagel caves.

15
THE
DEAL

Even though she'd been back home in Brixton for over two weeks Joanna still had recurring nightmares about the dead dragon. Sometimes she was flying on Excelsior and they were being chased by a dragon that could slash though rocks with its enormous razor-sharp claws. In another dream she was lying on the beach unable to move, slowly suffocated by the sweet stench of its decaying body. One night she even dreamt that Excelsior was the dead dragon, his skull lying crushed and bloodied on the sand.

Worst of all was sensing Excelsior's own fear when she mind-blended. She'd never known him to be afraid, but he was now and she could feel it – like a deep low tremor resonating through his thoughts.

Everyone was very sympathetic. She'd even had a card from Hannibal.

When the WDRF autopsy finally came out a fortnight later Marion Claverdale, who was over from the States on WDRF business, brought it round to the Brixton Caves personally.

'I wanted you to see the full report before you saw it anywhere else. I've been told it'll be in the evening's paper and on the news,' she said to Jo, who was sitting with Spiky Mike in his office.

Joanna took the report from Marion and immediately started to read the first page. But all it told her was that an unknown dragon – a male, one year old – had been discovered dead on a beach in North Wales. Cause of death: crushed skull with secondary injuries of lacerations to wings and belly.

This wasn't anything she didn't know already. More frustratingly, nobody seemed to be taking seriously her claim that she had seen similar claws on a dragon at the Tintagel Caves.

'Why is there no mention of the dragon I saw at Tintagel? My aunt saw it too ' questioned Joanna

Marion Claverdale was trying to be sympathetic as she could, but now she spoke quite sternly to Joanna.

'Your aunt has no recollection of a dragon with "terrible" claws. Joanna, you weren't yourself at Tintagel – remember you had nearly fainted . . .'

'That's because I picked up another dragon's fear! And there was this other angry dragon . . .'

Jo turned to her trainer.

'Spiky Mike, you believe me don't you?'

'You *are* very sensitive at picking up dragon's thoughts . . .' was all he'd say.

Joanna stood up slowly. 'Yeah, well, thanks for bringing the report.'

'Try and put it behind you, Joanna,' said Marion Claverdale, her voice softening. 'You've got a challenging season coming up. Hannibal is training hard and you'll need to be on top form to beat him. It would be a shame if this incident got in the way.'

Joanna left Spiky Mike to see Marion out and wandered down to Vincent's study. There was a light on. Was Isaac there?

It wasn't Isaac; it was her tutor Mr Hogan, who told her that Isaac had gone to see a film with a friend.

Oh. He hadn't invited her. She felt a stab of disappointment. Did Isaac think she'd lost the plot too? Joanna was turning to go when she decided to ask Mr Hogan's advice.

'Mr Hogan, what would you do if you saw something and nobody else believed you?'

Mr Hogan thought for a moment.

'I would go over the facts as I saw them. And then weigh the probability of them being true or me being mistaken. I'd also consider how important the incident was and what I would gain or lose from arguing my case. If I felt it was important, I would try and find further evidence to support it.'

'Thank you,' said Joanna thoughtfully. 'That's really helpful.'

Amber Penhaligon was very pleased to be back at her mother's house in West London. Already a whole month had gone by since she'd witnessed the fight club on the beach. So much had happened since then and now the time had come to share her fantastic news.

As soon as the doorbell rang, Amber quickly checked her appearance in the mirror in the hall, applied a quick dab of lip-gloss, flicked her hair and opened the door.

'Hey Isaac, you found the house OK?'

Isaac followed Amber into the sitting room.

'We'll need to go soon if we're going to catch the start of the film.'

Amber turned to him, her eyes shining with excitement.

'Do you mind if we skip the film? I've got some *awesome* news, and I'm too excited to think about anything else.'

Isaac shrugged his shoulders.

'I'm easy. Go on.'

'Do you remember Diego, the Scarlet Spiked-Back we saw in San Francisco? He's not in San Francisco any more.' Amber flicked her hair and gave a dazzling smile. 'He arrived here in London. Today!'

Isaac reacted as she hoped he would and wanted to know all the details, especially how she'd managed to get her dad to agree to her racing.

Amber proudly announced she had a sponsor who was paying for everything, so her dad didn't have to worry about the expense of it all – which had been one of his main concerns. And Jamie had promised he'd keep a close eye on her and had hired one of the WDRF caves over in Wimbledon, where he worked.

'And tomorrow I'm going to see Ms Lupin to arrange for my flying gear. I'm glad we've got decent colours for our cave – silver, red and midnight blue. There's going to be an official announcement in the next edition of *Dragon Fire*, so don't tell anyone until then, because I want it to be a big surprise!'

Isaac was suitably impressed about everything and promised to come and visit Diego the following Saturday.

'And you must come and see me race.'

Isaac looked unsure.

'I don't go to the races very often. I might make it up to Blackpool for the Novice Race. I've always wanted to go. The dragon is due to hatch mid-October and I'll be free for a few more weeks before we get a new batch of eggs.'

Amber slipped her arm through Isaac's.

'Ooh I'd love to watch your dragon hatch! What do you have to do?'

'Watch and wait and . . .'

Isaac stopped for a moment. Amber smiled.

'Do you have a secret egg turning trick up your sleeve? Is it that silver fire you made when you saved all those dragons from the flu?'

'That's the plan,' said Isaac.

'Can I come and watch?'

Amber looked at Isaac. He shook his head.

'Fraid not.'

'Because of Joanna? Not sure she likes me too much.'

'Jo can be tricky sometimes, admitted Isaac. 'But think what's happened to her in the past couple of years, and once you get to know her she's great.' He smiled sheepishly. 'You can't come to watch because of *me*!' He laughed when she pulled a face. 'I have to concentrate!'

'Oh and you couldn't if I was there.' Amber smiled and flicked her hair.

It was only after Isaac had gone home that Amber let out a huge sigh of relief. That had all gone much better than she'd planned. She'd expected him be full of the news report about the dead dragon that Joanna had found. But he hadn't even mentioned it.

When the news had first broken Amber realised immediately it was the dragon she'd seen killed. Not that she had a clue how sea currents worked, or even where the dead dragon had been dumped in the sea. She was sure that the fight would be discovered and was so worried for Jamie that even though she was still furious with him she decided to speak to him again to try and persuade him to stop.

It was what had happened next that was so extraordinary. She had burst into Galahad's caves, where she knew he was giving the dragon a claw trim before he headed back to London.

'Jamie, I know about the dragon fights! I think we need to talk.' She said it quickly, so he couldn't interrupt. But it wasn't her brother in the cave – it was Dr Braithwaite.

Dr Braithwaite didn't seem concerned at all at her outburst.

'What is there to talk about?' he replied evenly.

Amber glowered angrily. 'Just leave my brother alone.'

Dr Braithwaite laughed. 'Your brother is quite big enough to make his own decisions.'

'But Joanna Morris has found the dead dragon and there'll be an investigation . . .'

'Ah yes, our little world champion,' said Dr

Braithwaite. 'I hear you know her?'

Amber found it impossible to conceal her dislike for Joanna, especially her annoying habit of fainting to get attention. And that she so obviously had a problem with Amber being friends with Dominic and Isaac.

Dr Braithwaite's response was most unexpected.

'I'm surprised *you* don't race.'

Amber launched into a tirade against her dad and how he was always going on about how expensive racing was and the importance of her education and a trillion other excuses . . . She stopped. Why did Dr Braithwaite care? This was a man who enjoyed watching dragons die horrible cruel deaths. She started to make her excuses and turned to leave, when he suddenly spoke again.

'Of course, you *could* race if you had a sponsor. Someone your family could trust . . . someone like me.'

Amber stood still in her tracks. His tone was clear. Sponsorship – if she kept quiet about the dragon fight. He was blackmailing her. What should she do? He must be seriously worried she'd tell and she would indeed shop Dr Braithwaite at the drop of a hat – but Jamie?

And at last here was her opportunity to race . . . She turned back slowly to face Dr Braithwaite.

He smiled. 'I'm sure Jamie will be very proud to

see his sister racing and I'll have a word with your father.' Then he hesitated. 'I do have one further tiny request. There's some information I want you to find out for me.'

So here she was, entered for the season with a dragon to fly and training in London. All she had to do was find out from Isaac some information on this silver flame thing. How hard could it be?

16
CRUSHED

A few days later, after her morning's lessons were over, Joanna hurried down to Excelsior's cave, desperate to discuss an incident from earlier in the day. At least Excelsior took her concerns seriously. They'd talked endlessly about how Joanna could prove the dragon on the beach was the same one she'd seen at the Penhaligon Caves. Or whether lots of dragons had claws like that. And why nobody else fainted when dragons were in distress. She wished she could talk to Isaac about things too, but she hardly saw him and when she did he seemed so distracted and never stopped to chat.

Actually it was Isaac she wanted to discuss. That morning she'd found the door to Vincent's study wide open, the lights blazing and a pile of books open on the floor. It could only have been Isaac who'd left it in such a mess, as Mr Hogan hadn't arrived for the day yet. Isaac was usually meticulous at leaving everything tidy.

Excelsior put it down to Isaac being nervous about hatching out his first dragon egg.

'It's just a couple of weeks away now – he's probably swotting up on all sorts of technical details.'

'I can't wait to see the new dragon hatch,' said Joanna. 'When Aurora was born I couldn't believe anything could be so lovely and perfect. I just wanted to pick her up and cuddle her. I still can't believe she's not here . . .'

Excelsior shook his head. 'Talk about something else.'

Joanna nodded understandingly. 'I wonder what names Isaac is thinking of? Hope it's not after some footballer. That's what my brother suggested last night. Imagine if he called it Beckham!'

The day of the dragon hatching, October the fourteenth, arrived at last. Joanna hurried down the stairs to the cave, knowing that Isaac would be busy preparing the fire in the great fireplace in Vincent's study. He'd been given permission to have the day off school especially for the hatching. Not for the first time was Joanna grateful for her unusual education with Mr Hogan, who considered watching a dragon being born as important as understanding Pythagoras's theorem.

She was so absorbed in her thoughts that she bumped straight into Isaac coming up the stairs. He pushed past her without saying anything.

'Isaac!'

She turned to see Spiky Mike following Isaac.

'Not now Jo, crisis here,' he snapped and disappeared up the stairs after Isaac.

Joanna met Mr Hogan wheeling his chair out of Vincent's study. He was looking concerned, too.

'Mr Hogan, what's happened?' Joanna ran up to her teacher.

'Poor Isaac. He's been waiting so long for this moment. I don't understand it at all.'

'Mr Hogan,' asked Joanna, more worried and confused than ever. 'Has something happened to the egg?'

'Not the egg.' Mr Hogan could barely speak. '*Spiritus draconis* – the silver fire . . . Isaac says he can't make it.'

Joanna rushed past Mr Hogan into Vincent's study. She went over to the fireplace. Isaac had told her he just had to think of things he loved and the fire came as easy as breathing. Joanna closed her eyes and remembered how she'd seen Isaac ablaze with the silver fire when he'd saved Excelsior. So why not now?

She didn't understand. Isaac loved that egg.

Mr Hogan had wheeled his chair back into the study.

'Joanna, is anything troubling Isaac?

Joanna turned back to Mr Hogan and shook her head.

'He hasn't said, but then I've hardly seen him.'

Mr Hogan went over to the desk and turned on his laptop.

'Nothing more we can do for now. I'll just stay in the study and get on with the next translation. Isaac and I are already three quarters of the way through translating Vincent's manuscripts – though they don't look quite as beautiful in a Word document. We've been working so hard trying to understand it all . . .' his voice trailed off. Joanna could see how upset Mr Hogan was.

'Mr Hogan, I don't think it's your fault.'

'Can't make the fire?' Excelsior was astounded. 'But it's like your heart beating – you don't think about it, it's just there.'

He breathed out a beautiful shimmering silver flame.

'That's for you by the way.'

Immediately Joanna felt a deep, affectionate warmth wrap round her.

'Can you do that for me too, XL?' called a low voice from the cave entrance.

Isaac came in. His eyes looked small and red. Had he been crying?

'I mean it.' Isaac voice cracked. 'Will you hatch out the egg . . . in the silver fire for me . . . Just because I've messed up . . . doesn't mean the new . . . dragon should suffer.'

Excelsior reply was gruff and to the point. 'Go and get the egg.'

Isaac returned, quickly followed by Spiky Mike with Afra and Hannibal, just arrived from Brighton. Joanna was pleased to see them, though she wasn't sure Isaac was. He looked so crushed kneeling next to the firebox, which had housed the egg for the past fourteen months.

'Wait for me!' Mr Hogan came into the cave, positioning his chair next to Excelsior. 'I've never seen a dragon hatch.'

Isaac's hands were trembling as he lifted up the lid to reveal a golden speckled egg cradled in a pale blue flame.

'I can't believe this is the last time I'll see the egg. I know every line and speckle on its shell. See that dark gold bit at the top? That's been spreading and getting darker for the last month. And if I twist it to the right the dragon inside flips over to get comfy again.' He gave a small laugh. 'I love this egg you know, silly isn't it?'

'Course not,' Joanna sank down next to him. 'You've guarded and protected it, as if it were part of you.'

'Then why can't I make the silver fire, Jo?' He turned to her with such sadness on his face that she didn't know what to say.

'To everything there is a season and a time for every purpose under heaven.' A different voice came from the doorway.

'Grandma!' Isaac turned to look up to see Agnes, the old egg-turner.

'I couldn't miss my grandson hatching out his first egg. But it's no time for tears. I understand you can't make the silver fire, but there's a job that needs doing.'

'I've asked Excelsior to make the fire for me,' said Isaac flatly.

'Better get a move on or it'll have hatched before you're ready,' commented his grandma.

Isaac gave a loud sniff.

'Ready, XL?' He turned a knob on the side of the firebox and the blue flame instantly died A moment later the egg was covered in a fierce, bright, silver light as Excelsior bathed it in fire. The twisting flames looked like an exotic flower. Joanna felt herself hypnotised by its light. It seemed no time at all since she had been sitting there waiting for the last egg to hatch, giving birth to the beautiful, gentle Aurora. She looked up at Excelsior. She could feel his excitement at hatching the new egg was tinged with a wistful sadness for his old friend. Kneeling beside her, Isaac was staring so hard at the egg she thought his eyes would bore a hole in the shell. Agnes, with her years of experience, smiled at his anxious face.

'Patience.'

Just when Joanna thought it would never happen, small cracks appeared on the surface of the egg, fracturing its shell into a myriad of tiny fragments, so that it looked as though it was dissolving in front of their eyes. In its place, basking in the heat of the flame, coiled and still, lay a golden dragon. It looked slowly around as if surprised to be born. Before it had chance to move, Isaac picked up the startled creature and carefully placed him in the waiting glass cabinet. For a moment nobody said anything as they waited for Isaac to speak. He looked at them all blankly.

'So, Isaac.' Agnes was not allowing her grandson to wallow in self-pity. 'What is it? Girl or boy?'

'Boy,' replied Isaac quietly.

Joanna couldn't contain her excitement any longer.

'His name . . . Oh what's he called? He's beautiful. Look how smooth and small his scales are. And I love the dark gold spikes.'

The dragon suddenly came to life. Spreading his wings, he tried to fly out of the cabinet. It was then they all saw his back legs. Around each ankle was a frill of skin, like a small wing.

At last Isaac laughed. 'I've just changed my mind. I was going to name him . . .'

'No, don't say it,' interrupted Joanna. 'Just tell us his name *now*.'

'Hermes,' said Isaac. 'The winged messenger.'

'Hermes was a bit of a trickster too,' laughed Mr Hogan. 'Could be useful in the racing world.'

The dragon obviously heard as he somehow managed to push the lid off the cabinet and flew out into the cave.

'Just think – I was that small when I met you,' said Excelsior to Joanna, who was watching in delight as Hermes swooped around the roof of the cave.

'As long as Hermes doesn't give us the same trouble you did when it comes to choosing a flyer,' replied Spiky Mike grinning broadly and looking very pleased with the new dragon. He turned to Isaac. 'Come on, let's get the paperwork sorted and then I suggest we all go out for a celebratory lunch. I don't know about you, but I'm starving.'

Excelsior gave a huge snort. 'Hey, who did all the work?!'

17
SECRETS

Joanna left the restaurant with little sense of it being a celebration. Hannibal had upset her saying his main reason for being up in London was because he had an interview with *Dragon Fire* the following day. And as for Isaac, he didn't say a word to anyone. He'd ordered spaghetti bolognese but instead of eating it, he sat there twirling the pasta only to then let it slowly unwind. Then he just got up and left, saying he wanted to tidy up the egg turning cave before starting the evening feeds as he was going out later on and wanted a prompt getaway.

Joanna was heading home when she caught sight of Isaac crossing over the road in the high street. In a split moment decision she decided to follow him. It was mad thing to do, but she couldn't lose the opportunity to find out what was going on with Isaac. Brixton was already busy with the Friday rush hour and in such a crowd of people she could easily get away unnoticed. She was small, and Isaac tall. If she stayed far enough back, surely he wouldn't see her. She followed him down the steps of the underground, relieved she had remembered to bring her Oyster card. There was a train on the platform and she stood at the far end of the carriage from him, hiding as best she could by pretending to read a newspaper left on one of the seats. But soon she felt she could have been standing right in front of him and he wouldn't have realised she was there. He'd plugged in his earphones and sat motionless with his eyes closed until Oxford Circus, where she nearly lost him. At the last minute he'd seemed to realise where he was and jumped up off the train into a huge crowd of shoppers. She caught sight of him heading off in the direction of the Central Line.

The platform was packed but she slipped through the crowds and on to the train behind him. Squashed behind a man in a large black overcoat, she began to wonder what she was doing in the Friday rush hour, hiding from one of her best friends, on a train that was rattling off into the darkness towards West London. Station after station passed by and still Isaac just sat there. Eventually he stood slowly up. He must be getting off. So where were they? She craned her neck to see the sign. *Holland Park.* Underneath that the words, *Lift to street this way.* There was a crush of bodies waiting, but, even so, there would be nowhere to hide in a lift.

Joanna eyed the emergency stairs. How long would they take? She risked losing him for good, but there wasn't much choice. She charged up, ignoring the stitch in her side and the ache in her calves, bursting out at the top just as the lift doors opened. Isaac was first out and through the ticket barrier.

Following Isaac into the street, Jo managed to stay behind the man in the black overcoat she'd hidden behind earlier. Isaac took the second left. She ran to the corner of the road he'd gone down and peeped round, just time to see him climbing the steps and disappearing through the front door of a very smart, three-storey house. Joanna made her way up the street, careful to stay in the shadows of the trees, and stood opposite. The door flew open again. Joanna turned her face quickly away and was about to run back to the main road, when she heard a voice she recognised.

'No he doesn't know I've been here. I'll find the right time to tell him . . . not yet.'

Afra! And she was walking down the steps with . . . *Jamie Penhaligon*!

Jamie got into the car beside Afra and they drove off into the London evening.

Joanna was too shocked to move. Afra and Jamie!

What should she do? Poor Spiky Mike! Should she tell him? And the very person she would have talked it through with was already in the house the pair had come from. Had he seen Afra there? She could hardly ask Isaac without him revealing she'd followed him. On top of that, she now knew very well why Isaac hadn't been spending as much time in Brixton. There, in the front window, was Amber.

Joanna trudged back to the station in a sort of daze. Her head was in a spin. That Isaac was seeing Amber was bad enough, but Afra! Her words were on a constant replay in Joanna's head.

'No he doesn't know I've been here. I'll find the right time to tell him . . . not yet.'

How could she face her trainer? She knew too much, but at the same time not enough. Right on cue her phone buzzed with a message.

Where r u? CALL ME NOW. It was her mum.

Joanna's thumb hovered over the call button. She knew she should reply. But she wasn't ready to talk to *anybody*. She quickly texted Back soon J x

All the way home on the train she went over and over thinking what to do. How could these Penhaligons have such a hold over her friends that they became like strangers to her?

Her mum was furious when she got back home.

'A simple phone call, Joanna. I didn't have a clue where you were.'

'Sorry, Mum, look can we talk about it tomorrow . . .' Joanna got a glass of orange from the fridge. 'I've . . . fallen out with Isaac . . .' (Why had she said that?) Before her mum could put on her questioning face Joanna got up and walked out of the kitchen. 'I really don't want to talk about it.'

Joanna was dreading Monday morning even after a weekend of being grounded, which was made worse when her brother came home having seen Isaac at football practice and told their parents that Isaac and Joanna *hadn't* fallen out.

To Joanna's surprise, Spiky Mike seemed fine. She heard him whistling – always a sign he was in a good mood – and he looked quite normal – jeans, T-shirt from some favourite band. He'd even had a shave. No designer stubble this morning.

'Hey, Jo, got a favour to ask you. Afra and I invited Ms Lupin down to Brighton this weekend to discuss the uniform for our school.' Joanna pulled a face. She still hated the thought of having to share her trainer with anyone else.

Spiky Mike ignored her grimace. 'Lotty has got some great ideas, but we're really keen that you and Isaac should take a look. Afra likes the navy blue, but I like the maroon. How about a trip up to Lupin Designs to look at our ideas? It'll have to be after school sometime this week so that Isaac can come too.'

'OK,' said Joanna, thinking that it wasn't as if Mr Hogan would let her skip lessons to get her outfit either. 'Any day's fine with me. And my new racing gear's ready, so I can get that, too.'

'Go and ask Isaac – he's down with Hermes – then I can let Lotty and Afra know.' Spiky Mike turned back to his laptop. 'And hurry up – this morning I want to start rehearsing your showpiece for Blackpool.'

Now wasn't the time to talk about Afra.

Isaac wasn't with Hermes; he was in Vincent's study, tidying up the main bookshelf.

'Hi,' said Joanna. 'Do you need some help?'

Isaac continued what he was doing without looking at Joanna.

'What's all this about you and me having an argument?'

'It was just an answer to get my mum off my back,' said Joanna, blushing. 'I was late back on Friday and hadn't let her know. Anyhow trust my blubber mouth brother to stir things. Did you have a good weekend?' she managed to add without her voice shaking too much.

'Yeah, it was great to get back to football.' He righted the last book. 'I've got to get off to school now.'

'Before you go,' said Joanna. 'Spiky Mike asked if you could come up to Ms Lupin's after school this week and look at designs for the Brighton school uniform?'

Isaac climbed down off the stool and shook his head.

'I don't think so . . . I might as well tell you now that I'm taking a break . . . I'll just be in to do the feeding.' He pointed up at the bookshelves. 'Don't worry; I've put all the books back properly.' And he picked up his school bag and left.

If he'd actually hit her it couldn't have hurt more. Even if he was *gutted* about not being able to make the silver fire, surely he couldn't just walk away like that? Joanna didn't recognise this Isaac and she didn't know what to do as the twisted knot in her stomach gave way to a sob of tears.

18
FIGHT
BACK

Excelsior went wild with fury. He stormed round and round his cave, flapping his wings, flaring his nostrils and breathing out a flare of bright red fire. Joanna had never seen him so angry.

'He can't just walk away. *I'm* a dragon, *you* are a flyer and *he* is the Alchemist. Full stop! Why do humans have to make things so complicated?'

'But he's upset at not being able to make the silver fire.' Joanna didn't know why she found herself excusing Isaac.

'And whose fault is that? No one but his own.'

'What?' Joanna was completely taken aback.

'*Ignem amore accende!* – Light the fire with love. Something is preoccupying, taking him away from what he truly cares about. And the only thing that I can see that has changed is . . .'

'. . . Amber.' Joanna finished off his sentence dejectedly.

'So tell him!' said Excelsior matter of factly.

'I can't do that,' exclaimed Joanna.

'What! You can't tell him the truth?'

'Sometimes facing the truth is the most difficult thing ever,' said Joanna sadly. 'Like the fact he likes Amber and not me.'

'A passing fancy, nothing more. No reason for you to keep the truth secret,' replied Excelsior fiercely. 'If you ask me, secrets lead to trouble.'

'What if it's not your secret? I discovered something else on Friday night . . . something terrible. About Afra. And I don't know whether I should tell Spiky Mike.'

'Tell me what, Jo?'

Joanna turned round aghast to see Spiky Mike himself staring down at her. He looked worried, amused and curious all at the same time. Joanna swallowed hard.

'I think you should talk to Afra,' she said.

Spiky Mike didn't move, but stood looking at his young flyer as she twitched from foot to foot.

Joanna felt Excelsior's thought nudging her. *Best get it said.*

She avoided telling him about following Isaac. It was horrible having to say she'd seen Afra and Jamie driving off together. Joanna found she couldn't bear to look at her trainer. When she did look up Spiky Mike didn't seem as upset as she had expected.

'You guessed he's an old boyfriend of Afra's, did you? I saw those looks between you and Mouse. I don't like the guy, and I don't like the way he is around Afra. Plain old-fashioned jealousy, I guess. But there's nothing suspicious about Afra being there. She'd gone to get a special prescription because Ebony's developing phlegm on her chest. Brighton is damp and chilly after California. We didn't want Hannibal worrying – not after last season and everything with Aurora – so we thought we'd get it sorted whilst he was up in London this weekend. The medicine worked. She's fine.'

Joanna didn't know whether to laugh or cry she was so relieved.

'You won't tell Afra will you?'

'I won't say a word,' said Spiky Mike with an uncharacteristic sling of his arm round Joanna's shoulder. 'How about we go down to the training cave and start work on the Novice Race opening display? Or we *will* have something to worry about!'

Joanna hardly saw Isaac over the next few days. He was as good as his word, only coming in to feed the dragons. Mr Hogan was philosophical about it.

'Only natural, given the circumstances. In the

meantime, I'll continue with my translations of Vincent's manuscripts. You don't want to help me do you?'

Joanna looked in horror at her teacher, until she realised he was just teasing her. Still, Joanna found the caves a lonely place without her friend. She was pleased she had the visit to Ms Lupin's to look forward to.

Late Friday afternoon Afra arrived at the Brixton Caves to take Joanna up to the studios in Mayfair.

'Girls' afternoon,' smiled Afra. 'Mike's idea. Thought we'd enjoy it more. But can you remind me that I've got to get him a new pair of gloves? He's always complaining about how cold his fingers get at the early morning training sessions.'

Joanna was pleased to hear Afra talking like her mum would about her dad. Ordinary couple stuff.

She hadn't been up to Lupin Designs since the previous Christmas and it was looking very different. Gone was the pink tree; instead, a golden dragon fountain filled the entrance hall. The white leather sofa at reception was piled high with bright, fiery cushions, in orange, red and gold. On the wall a huge poster announcing the new Autumn Collection, *Breath of Fire*, showed tall elegant models dressed in one-piece racing suits in shimmering bronze, copper and dark ochre.

'I love the new all-in-one suits in vogue at the moment,' said Afra, coming up to look too.

'They're proving very popular this season,' Ms Lotty Lupin herself suddenly appeared from out of a doorway. She was wearing a long metallic bronze jumper dress, with matching dark leggings and high heel shoes. Her dark brown hair was tied up in a long French plait. It was simple and chic. Joanna wished she could look just like her.

'Could I wear my hair like that under my helmet? I'm really fed up of wearing it in two plaits.'

'Too school girly for you now,' laughed Ms Lupin.

'I'll braid it for you if you like,' said Afra. 'We can experiment to get just the right look.'

Ms Lupin smiled. 'Looks like you've just acquired a personal hairdresser, Jo. Ready to see your new suit? The new crystal beading's already attracted a lot of attention and I have lots of requests for something similar.'

Joanna loved visiting Ms Lupin's studio, with its baskets of sequins, rhinestones and ribbons, the noticeboards of sketches and swatches of fabric. Today there was a rail with four outfits.

'Here's Hannibal's. I've just finished it.'

Ms Lupin took down a black suit with a gold studded outline of a sparkling black dragon.

'I love this one,' Joanna pointed to the suit next to it. It was a deep midnight blue; the cuffs, neck and back of the jacket were covered in tiny crystal beads that twinkled as they caught the light.

'Take it down, have a look. I used the new crystal beads on that one too. It's for another new young racer, this is her first season.'

'I hadn't heard there was another girl racing,' said Joanna. 'How exciting. Who is she?'

'She was a very late entry. Her name's Amber Penhaligon. Pretty girl.'

Joanna's heart sank. That was all she needed. She took down the suit. Written in sparkling letters was Amber's name - confirmation indeed that Amber was enrolled as a flyer for the current season. But what was this underneath her name? Joanna stared at the image of two dragons fighting. A red dragon crushing a silvery white one.

'Interesting choice of design, Lotty,' said Joanna as casually as should could.

'The two dragons are a reference to an Arthurian legend,' explained Ms Lupin. 'Amber asked for it especially.'

That's what she wants you to think, thought Joanna, *but I rather think it's a direct challenge to me.* Joanna smiled to herself as she put the suit back on the rack and took down her own, its sparkling silver dragon soaring with outspread wings. She was ready for Amber's challenge.

19
HERMES

Isaac squatted down next to Hermes. The golden dragon was about the size of a Labrador and seemed far too small to live alone in such a huge cave. He was snuffling around his legs, looking for food.

'Not time yet, greedy,' said Isaac crossly. 'I heard about you causing havoc down in Brighton, trying to get into the food supplies at midnight, and setting off all the alarms.'

He pushed the dragon away harshly and Hermes let out a yelp as he flew off to hide on the ledge of an air duct at the top of the cave. Hermes had already loosened the wire mesh and Isaac could only hope the dragon wouldn't want to go exploring.

'Sorry, fella. I just don't know what's the matter with me. Come back down here. Look, I've got a treat for you.'

He took a minced chicken biscuit from his pocket and the dragon swooped down to swallow it in one gulp. Hermes looked up hopefully with his great golden eyes.

Isaac stared back as if trying to see inside the dragon's skull. Only a short time ago he'd known every mark and spot of Hermes' eggshell, but now that he was born it was as though he didn't know the dragon at all. Isaac ran his fingers over the crown of sharp spines on the top of Hermes' head.

'I could tell with just a twist of the egg how you were lying; if you were sleeping or agitated. You would have thought I'd find it the easiest thing in the world to make the fire for you. But I couldn't . . .'

To Isaac's surprise Hermes answered. The dragon's voice was as high and squeaky as Isaac had always imagined it to be.

'You turned my egg, but *I* don't hold the answer – you'll have to look inside yourself. Turn yourself over as you turned me.'

'Easier said than done, Hermes.'

Isaac sat down with his back to the wall and closed his eyes. He should really go and feed Excelsior. Joanna would be back soon from Ms Lupin's and he wanted to avoid seeing her because . . . seeing her reminded him how he'd failed.

He traced the letters on the floor of the cave. How many times had he said those words, or even just thought them? It felt like they were inscribed on his brain. *Just feel it, Isaac*, he said to himself. *You know it's there*. But that was the trouble – he didn't know any more *what* he felt . . . except confusion.

'I wish I could just get away from it all!' he cried out loud. 'Just fly away and not have to think, or feel.'

Hermes came up to his side. 'Why not fly, then?'

Isaac didn't reply but stood there thinking for a moment until a smile slowly spread across his face.

'Think I'll go and have a chat with Spiky Mike . . . thanks Hermes, you've just given me a brilliant idea.'

'I'm going to learn to fly a dragon!'

Isaac walked into Excelsior's cave.

Joanna turned round from oiling Excelsior's wings. She couldn't believe it. Isaac was actually smiling!

'I've been a bit of an idiot, Jo – still am, I reckon. Hermes said I should learn to fly. So I went to see Spiky Mike and he suggested I go up to Wales at half-term.'

'Isaac, that's really brilliant. You'll love it, it's the best.' Joanna was genuinely pleased. (Never mind that Amber would be nowhere near the Snowdonia Dragon Sanctuary . . .)

'And Giovanni's going to bring me over to watch the Novice Race in Blackpool. We can all drive back together!'

Joanna's eyes shone with delight.

'You'll be able to take part in the 'Fly by Night' before the race. I can't wait!'

Isaac smiled back. Neither could he.

'Oh, by the way,' Jo carried on. 'If they ask you, the school uniform for Brighton needs to be in navy blue, not the awful maroon Spiky Mike wants.'

Isaac was about to go when he caught sight of *Dragon Fire* magazine sticking out of Joanna's bag. It was still sealed in its plastic wrapping.

'Is that the new season edition?' asked Isaac. 'Can I have a quick look?'

'Sure,' said Joanna. She suddenly stopped. Of course, there would be a full listing of all the novice flyers and novice dragons. Amber would be in it. She watched Isaac flick quickly past a full-page article on Hannibal, but not before she glimpsed the headline, *Friend or Foe.*

'The new flyers are always in a centre pull-out. Here . . .'

She took the magazine and pulled out the centre-fold, causing a whole avalanche of adverts and vouchers to tumble out on to the floor.

'I hear Amber's flying this season,' said Joanna. 'Although I expect you know that already. I saw her suit yesterday at Ms Lupin's.'

Amber's photo was next to Dominic's. Joanna was struck with how good-looking they both were. She wondered if Isaac was thinking the same thing. But what he said surprised her.

'Look at all the new dragons. Makes you realise how many died in the flu outbreak.'

It was true. So many flyers' lives turned upside down by Marius King – their beautiful dragons, their best friends, gone forever. She breathed in sharply, and then looked about for something to distract her thoughts.

'Are there any good vouchers?' she asked a bit too brightly, picking up the pile on the floor. 'Sometimes they have a two-for-one deal for the fun fair in Blackpool.'

Isaac pulled out one of Blackpool Tower next to a QR code. He took out his phone. 'I've got an app for these.'

But the website page had nothing to do with the fun fair or Blackpool Tower. It was just a picture – a geometric pattern with one red triangle and one white on a black background.

'Probably one of those obscure advertising gimmicks,' said Isaac. 'Trying to be all mysterious and in the end it's some fizzy drink they're launching at the race.'

But Joanna wasn't listening. She'd been distracted by an article on the back page of the magazine.

'Isaac, listen to this - it's awful!' Joanna started to read. '*Attack at Devil's Slide Caves. A dragon being kept in a secure unit for observation has viciously attacked an intern during a routine check-up at the Heywood Consortium in California, USA. The intern sustained life-threatening injuries and is in hospital on a life-support machine. Managing director Cliff Heywood has ordered an immediate review of safety policy.'*

'Poor guy!' said Isaac.

Joanna sat there in silence, obviously with something on her mind.

'What?' said Isaac apprehensively.

'Do you remember when I fainted at the Devil's Slide Caves?'

'Can't really forget . . .' said Isaac, a little more scathingly than he'd intended.

'Never mind . . . it's nothing, just me being silly again,' said Joanna, hurt by Isaac's comment.

She picked up the magazine and gave it to Isaac. 'Here, borrow it if you want. Just leave it on Vincent's desk when you've finished. I think it's brilliant about you learning to fly.'

When Isaac had gone Joanna turned to Excelsior, who had watched the whole thing in silence.

They both knew what she was thinking. Jo had sensed angry and frightened dragons at Tintagel and Devil's Slide. Now a dead dragon had turned up at one and a dragon had turned violent at the other. And which person linked the two places?

20
EXPECTATIONS

Amber threw the bucket on to the floor. Its metallic clang echoed off the cave walls. Her dragon, Diego, looked over at her, unconcerned by her outburst.

'Come on, the session wasn't that bad. Our take-off was good and, with a time like that, we're in with a chance of a medal next week.'

Amber kicked the bucket itself this time. Diego's cool, laid back approach was starting to annoy her, especially after her trainer's scalding comments about *her* lack of depth in the mind-blend.

Racing was much harder than she'd expected. Every part of her body felt sore from being stuck in the flying position and her head ached from the concentration needed to sustain the mind-blend. On top of that there was all the grooming and feeding. She kicked the bucket again, this time making a small dent.

Amber hated the smell of the raw ground steak that Diego ate, particularly as she had to rinse it out after he had finished.

She decided to go and visit her brother for some tea and sympathy (and hopefully a lift home). His office was part of the same cave complex where she trained in Wimbledon. She found him busy reading the new season's edition of *Dragon Fire*.

'Can I see my photo?' She peered over his shoulder. But he was reading an article. *Attack at Devil's Slide Caves*.

Amber quickly scanned the article. The dragon had to be one used for fighting. She looked carefully at her brother. Did the article worry him? He wasn't acting like it did. She was sure he didn't suspect his sister knew his dark secret.

'So why are you here Amber?' he asked, putting down the magazine. 'Have you just come to steal my copy of *Dragon Fire*?'

Amber picked up a pen off his desk and started to doodle.

'I came for brotherly support. Looking after Diego is such hard work.'

To her dismay, Jamie wasn't at all sympathetic.

'What did you expect?' He snatched the pen from her hand and put it back down on his desk.

'You're always in a bad mood these days,' she moaned.

He pointed to a huge in-tray. 'It's called work, Amber. If you want to do something useful, give Dad a ring about driving Diego up to Blackpool for the Novice Race.'

'Aren't you driving me?' Amber looked surprised.

'I'm not here to chauffer you around all the time. I'm not coming up to Blackpool until the morning of the race. You'll need to be up a couple of days before to practise. What's wrong with Dad driving?'

Amber looked scornfully at her brother.

'He'll drive like a snail up the motorway, it'll take forever and when we do get there he'll have found some awful B&B to stay in.'

'*Actually* you are booked into a five-star hotel on the seafront, guests of Dr Braithwaite,' said Jamie, arching his eyebrows. 'He's invested a lot of money in you and Diego, so it's hardly surprising he wants to come and see how you are getting on. Now, phone Dad while I write out some prescriptions. *Then* I'll drive you home.'

Dr Braithwaite wants to check up on me. Amber didn't need her brother to tell her that. She knew from all the messages on her phone. She hadn't yet told Dr Braithwaite about Isaac turning up on her doorstep over a week ago in a terrible state. She'd tried to be sympathetic and listen, even asked questions – as much to pry out information as anything. Isaac had sat there not saying anything. In the end he'd just left. He seemed to have gone into some meltdown. He hadn't replied to any of her texts or calls, except to say he was going to some Welsh dragon sanctuary for half term.

Amber reluctantly phoned her father, then, as Jamie was still busy, picked up the copy of *Dragon Fire* to find her photo. Flyers were listed alphabetically, so she was sandwiched between Hannibal and Dominic. She was more than pleased to be seen alongside the next potential world champion. And she and Dominic could be models with their good looks. Perhaps Ms Lupin would invite her to do a photo shoot? She couldn't wait for the season to start!

21
FLY BY
NIGHT

The Blackpool Tower Caves were buzzing with flyers, dragons, trainers, press and WDRF officials.

'I'm so excited it's the start of the season,' beamed Joanna enthusiastically to a rather nervous reporter, who, being unused to dragons at such close quarters, kept anxiously eyeing up Hermes running between everyone's legs.

Joanna was posing for photographs when she saw Isaac. She was desperate to go over and interrogate him about his week in Wales, but she had to be content with a wave and a smile, before he was dragged away by Mouse for a game of football on the beach. Mouse gave a thumbs up and mouthed, 'Join us when you've finished.'

Joanna managed to escape when Hannibal and his mother arrived and they became the centre of the photographers' interest. (At least Hannibal acknowledged her and came to say hi.)

It was a wild and windy day and the tide was halfway in, but there was plenty of space left on the beach for football. Mouse had collected a whole gang of people and a game was in progress. Joanna ran down on to the hard flat sand shouting, 'Room for me?'

'Take my scarf, you need something red to show you're on our team,' answered Isaac, running past her with the ball. '*Dragon Racers* versus *Blackpool Rock Brigade* - or something like that.' He was tackled by a burly looking boy with blond hair and lost the ball.

'Hi Jo,' called a voice from behind her. She turned to see Dominic. Her tummy gave a flip on seeing him as he brushed his hair back off his face revealing his gorgeous green eyes. And he'd grown at least three inches over the summer. She was surprised and annoyed with herself at how pleased she was to see him.

They were beaten in the end by the tide. It swooped in at an alarming speed. There was still a good hour before they would have to prepare for the Fly by Night, so they went and bought fish and chips and sat on the prom. Someone had been busy flyposting the wall behind them with adverts for the races, including the mystery one with the QR code.

'Anyone know what this is advertising?' asked Joanna, pointing at the flyer.

Mouse pulled one off the wall and scanned it. '04 11 is today's date. So 21.00 must mean something happening at nine o'clock tonight. That's more or less the time the Fly by Night will finish, perhaps it's something to do with that.'

Joanna looked for a space to sit down. There was a space beside both Dominic and Isaac. Who should she choose? But then one of Mouse's school friends made the decision for her by plonking herself firmly down beside Dominic, desperate for him to sign her autograph book.

Joanna quickly sat down next to Isaac. He looked windswept and his dark eyes were bright and sparkling. He looked really happy.

'Wales . . . mountains . . . flying . . . I loved it. No wonder you're all hooked on it.' His dark face quivered for a second. 'And I learned to wait, to go with the flow, not to try too hard. Nia helped me. Made sure I didn't fall off. I might not ever make the fire again, but that's fine. I made it when it was really needed – that's what mattered.'

It was such a relief to see the real Isaac back again.

'Are you flying with us tonight?' asked Joanna.

'Try and stop me. Giovanni brought Nia especially. Apparently she's always wanted to see the Blackpool Illuminations.'

At seven o'clock a convoy of dragon transporters left the Blackpool Tower Dragon Caves and drove along the back road to the airport at Squires Gate – the traditional start for the Fly by Night. The runway was soon full of dragons and flyers, all jostling for space. The runway lights cast strange shadows of dragons with elongated necks and enormous wings.

'Let's fly together at the back, away from the crowd,' said Mouse. 'Ariadne can't fly that fast and likes lots of space.'

'Slow and at the back is perfect for me,' agreed Isaac. Excelsior blasted the cold night air with fire.

'I can do slow,' he insisted as Joanna climbed up on to his back. She looked around to see which flyers she recognised. Dominic had somehow got separated and was now in the middle of the pack. But there was only one person Joanna was interested in seeing. There she was – Amber, on the red dragon Diego. She was looking ahead and hadn't seen them.

An overhead loudspeaker sounded abruptly, calling all flyers to attention. Silence fell over the group. Nothing could be heard except the slow hiss of dragon breath, the metallic scraping of scale rubbing scale and the occasional clatter of claw on the tarmac as dragons steadied themselves for flight. And then they were off! The flight of dragons took to the air as one. A huge, leathery-winged swarm, they swung this way and that, gaining height before they set off to follow the famous Illuminations along the promenade. Far away to their left was the sea. The tide was going out again, nothing more than a soft roar beyond the blackness of the beach that stretched out for miles along the coast. All attention concentrated on the gaiety and fun below them.

'Best one yet,' exclaimed Mouse as they came in to land. 'My favourite was when the top of the tower went bright pink, and then turquoise blue. Hey Jo, did you see Ariadne loop the loop? We've been practising that move for ages.'

But Joanna didn't reply. She'd slipped off Excelsior and was staring out into the blackness of the beach. At least that was what it looked like to Mouse.

For Joanna, the night was burning up in angry twisted spirals of roaring red dragon fire. Her body was being crushed, forcing all the air out of her lungs so that she couldn't breathe and a sudden sharp stab of pain made her legs buckle beneath her. All around her she heard terrible shrieks and furious cries. She had to escape. She reached out wildly, clutching at Mouse, who was closest to her. Feeling the pain and chaos of his flyer, Excelsior panicked and took to the air, wings trembling and let out a huge deafening roar. All around chaos erupted as flyers screamed and ran in all directions as a few of the younger dragons followed Excelsior up into the sky.

Spiky Mike, waiting by the dragon transporter, quickly took in the situation and hurried forward.

'Don't run!' His voice was strong and firm. People stopped and listened. 'Control your dragon in a mind-blend,' he continued. 'And order them to fly slowly down in a clockwise motion.'

Soon Excelsior was left a solitary riderless dragon alone in the night sky, like a lost silvery ghost. Spiky Mike made his way over to Mouse and gave her a set of keys.

'Get Joanna back to the van, as fast as you can, whilst I sort out Excelsior.'

Joanna could barely stand, so Mouse looked around for someone to help her. She caught sight of Isaac. He was standing close to Nia, grateful that she hadn't taken to the skies.

'Isaac, over here, quick. I can't manage on my own,' Mouse called.

'Go and open the van door,' said Isaac as he scooped Jo up. She lay motionless and semi-conscious in his arms, staring up at him with wild eyes. What was she seeing?

Instinctively he closed his own eyes and thought gentle thoughts of everyday life in the Brixton Caves. This was what he did when he needed to feel calm.

Images flashed through his mind – feeding Excelsior, egg-turning, looking at the old manuscripts in Vincent's study.

And then, quite without warning, a flicker of silver flame flashed through him. Joanna gasped and her body jolted. Isaac stood there trembling. He'd made the silver fire! Had anyone else had seen? Isaac stood there unsure what to do next. He looked down at Joanna. Her eyes were focused now and looking up at his face. She half smiled.

'I'm OK – you can put me down.'

Isaac set her back on her feet. Neither of them moved until Mouse came running up.

'Let's get her to the van,' said Mouse. 'Come on Jo, me and Isaac will help you.'

But Joanna threw off her friend's arm.

'Really, I'm OK now. Isaac . . .?'

Isaac widened his eyes at her and shook his head almost imperceptibly, willing Jo not to tell Mouse what had just happened. That's if she had seen it . . .

She turned back to Mouse. 'I'm fine – I promise. I need to see XL's OK too.'

She ran over to where Spiky Mike was struggling to get Excelsior into the back of the transporter van. As soon as he had got everyone together her trainer drove them all back and sent them straight to bed. But being sent to bed was not the same thing as falling asleep. In fact it was highly questionable that the witnesses of the Silver Flame slept at all.

Joanna was awake, but peaceful. She could still feel the effects of the fire, but she could barely recall the terrible cries of the dragon that had distressed her so badly. She thought instead of being held safe in Isaac's arms.

Isaac was awake, but confused and hopeful. If the silver fire hadn't deserted him, what made it happen?

And Amber was awake. She'd seen the Silver Flame now with her own eyes. Seen how Isaac had shone with a brightness that made her shiver. Seen the look he gave Joanna.

22
READY WHEN
YOU ARE

Spiky Mike was in a dilemma. Should he let Joanna make her star appearance that afternoon? She had appeared bright and early the following morning, having slept well. She'd answered all his questions about what she had 'seen' the night before in a clear straightforward manner. She told him that Isaac had made the silver fire and that as a result she was feeling back to normal.

It was always possible she had picked up some dragon's thoughts, but it was more likely to be a reoccurring memory of the terrible incident in Wales . . . It was also the third time she'd fainted since the World Championships. He couldn't rule out that she was suffering from stress. To add to his worries, he'd also received three formal complaints that last night's incident had left flyers and dragons distressed the night before a major race.

In the end the decision was taken away from him. Marion Claverdale decided that whilst Joanna and Excelsior should still attend as guests of honour, the exhibition piece was to be cancelled.

Joanna was furious. 'I'm not ill. Something is happening to dragons. Why not ask Dr Penhaligon?' she shouted angrily. 'He's involved somewhere.'

Spiky Mike shook his head. 'I'm sorry about the exhibition piece, but even I can't believe you when you start accusing Jamie. The man only arrived in Blackpool this morning.'

That made Joanna stop in her tracks.

'Show everyone the champion you are,' said Spiky Mike. 'Don't make a fuss. Smile, present the medals, and . . .'

'And what? Have people think I can't fly because I'm having a breakdown?'

'But if you don't appear that is just what people will think,' said Spiky Mike arching his eyebrows.

'OK, you win,' sighed Joanna.

In the end, what helped was getting her hair done. Ms Lupin had sent up a stylist, not only to plait her hair, but also, to Joanna's delight, add some subtle golden highlights (something Joanna's mother had always refused to let Joanna do).

'Wow! Jo! Awesome!' said Mouse who had decided to assist Joanna as she changed into her racing suit.

Even though she wasn't flying, it seemed the most appropriate thing to wear.

Joanna turned this way and that in the mirror. In her new racing suit and with her new hairstyle, she hardly recognised herself. She couldn't help but smile she was so pleased.

'You show them!'

Mouse pushed her out of the changing rooms. The first person the girls met was Amber. She didn't say a word, but looked Joanna up and down, before walking quickly away.

Joanna's appearance caused quite a stir as she made her way up to the VIP enclosure, where she was going to watch the race. Hannibal just stared. Dominic came running up like a puppy dog wanting acknowledgement, and even Spiky Mike nodded in approval. Joanna looked around for Isaac. She hadn't seen him since the evening before. He was engrossed in reading the programme and hadn't looked up.

A fanfare announced the beginning of proceedings. Instead of Joanna's exhibition piece, they showed a rerun of Joanna's record-breaking race from the summer. Then Marion Claverdale and Joanna walked over to a small enclosure where Excelsior was waiting and from where Joanna would declare the racing season open. Joanna turned to face the spectators and gave a huge smile, aware that an army of cameras were filming her expression, which appeared huge on every screen. Were they hoping she would faint on camera?

'Ready when you are!' she beamed. 'Let's get this season underway.'

Conditions over the sea were far from perfect. There was low lying cloud and a stiff breeze as the flyers took their places. There were over twenty dragons taking part. Hannibal received a huge cheer from his enormous fan club and, to Joanna's surprise, Dominic seemed to be amassing a noisy fan club of his own.

The flyers mounted their dragons. The siren to start the mind-blend sounded. Everyone was silent, waiting . . . waiting for the race to start . . . and they were off.

Third time you've taken part in this race Hannibal, Hope you win this time, thought Joanna as the dragons flew up into the air. A classic, smooth take-off, careful positioning and a steady acceleration soon had Hannibal firmly out in front. At the halfway turn he rose higher in the sky, determined to out-manoeuvre any wayward dragons that might be headed his way. He certainly didn't want a repeat of last year's race when he crashed into Dominic on the turn. Joanna couldn't fault his tactics. So who would be second?

'Amber's chasing hard for second,' cried Isaac, rushing over to stand by Joanna. 'Come on Amber,' he called loudly.

'I can't see her overtaking Lucy Bell,' argued Joanna. 'Her new dragon Daiquiri looks fast.'

Experience paid off and Lucy Bell *just* managed to hold on to her second place. Still, Amber had come a close third.

Joanna began to make her way down to the winners' enclosure, annoyed at having to hand a medal to Amber of all people. She kept glancing up at the screens to watch as the novice flyers came into land. Dominic still hadn't finished. She stopped to look more carefully. A whole group of flyers were flying in together – and they were no longer racing. Something must be the matter.

Shouts and screams rippled out through the spectators. Everyone now was staring in horror at the huge viewing screens, mesmerised by the body of a dead dragon being carried along on the incoming tide. Its wings reminded Joanna of broken umbrellas and its front legs were twisted and bent. Joanna's tummy turned over at the memory of stinking rotting flesh. This must be the dragon she'd heard last night – she hadn't imagined it! The screens went blank as a crowd of WDRF officials could be seen hurrying over the sand to the water's edge.

Marion Claverdale was speaking at the microphone.

'Ladies and gentlemen, please remain in your seats while our officials take charge of the situation. Until we understand the circumstances behind this we can only ask for your cooperation and understanding. I promise you that the WDRF will make a statement as soon as we are able.'

Nobody was listening. There was uproar. Joanna was aware that Isaac was standing beside her, watching.

Joanna caught sight of Hannibal in the winners' enclosure looking severe. Beside him Ebony had her wings tightly folded to her body and her tail coiled round.

Joanna made her way over to him. 'I'm so sorry,' she said. 'There's always something that spoils things for you. It was brilliant flying.'

He didn't say very much, distracted by what was happening, so Joanna turned to Lucy Bell, who was standing close to her new dragon. Both of them were trembling from head to foot.

'Lucy, are you OK? Can I do anything to help?'

Lucy shook her head. 'I need to get Daiquiri back to her cave, but we've been told not to move.' Joanna could see Lucy was trying to fight back tears. 'I can't take another season like the last one.'

'I'll try and find out if you can go,' said Joanna as gently as she could. She turned to leave when Amber, who Joanna hadn't noticed until then, called over.

'Joanna, this is so awful. And it was such a brilliant race. Do you think we'll get our medals?'

Joanna couldn't believe her ears. A dead dragon had just turned up on the beach and all Amber was bothered about was whether or not she was going to get her medal? Didn't she have any idea how upset everyone was?

Down by the shore the dragon was being photographed by a team of forensic scientists, but the rising tide cut short their work and the dragon soon disappeared into the back of a transporter van to be driven hastily away. With nothing further to watch, the spectators quickly cleared the stands.

Soon there was only one person left watching. The wind had grown in strength and was whipping up white waves to pound the sea defences. On the promenade workmen were hastily dismantling the spectator stands and hospitality tents. Soon all traces of the afternoon race would be gone. Marius King breathed in deeply and smiled to himself. It was enough for now, that he had left his calling card – one dead dragon. He'd been quite pleased with the overall effect of his contribution to the afternoon's proceedings. Let everyone stew for a little, get upset that the season had got off to a bad start. It would be amusing to watch the WDRF try and explain the horror of *two* dead dragons. The trail would soon run cold, then when everyone had forgotten . . . then he would strike again. And next time it would be the grand finale!

23
MAKING FRIENDS WITH JOANNA

That evening Marion Claverdale called an emergency meeting of the top British WDRF officials attending the Blackpool race in the hotel lounge. They had to face the unwelcome truth that the dragon found on the beach had died from very unnatural causes.

'After an initial examination it appears the dragon died in a violent attack – probably killed by another dragon,' said Marion solemnly. 'Of course I am waiting for a more detailed report. I would also suggest that the appearance of a second dead dragon in the seas around the British Isles is not chance or coincidence, but evidence of something darker and more sinister.'

'How are you going to deal with the press?' asked the previous president, Sir John Miller, relieved it was Marion's problem and not his. Marion announced that she would be delaying her return to the States so that she could personally oversee the dreadful business.

I'll be announcing hard facts and details whenever I receive them, so as to keep any fabricated – and exaggerated – stories to a minimum,' declared Marion firmly. She had already ordered a full autopsy of the dragon, and had spoken to the Serious Organised Crime Agency to see if they have any intelligence as to who is behind all this.

An exhausted Marion was just on her way up to bed when she saw Jamie Penhaligon coming into the hotel lobby. She had ordered the vet to check the wellbeing of all the dragons taking part in the race. He gave her a quick wave.

'No need to worry Marion. Had to give a couple of dragons a mild sedative to help them sleep. Other than that, all is well.'

Marion came back down the stairs to talk to him.

'And how is Amber? Such a shame this happening on her first race.

'Amber taken it all in her stride.' replied Jamie with a hint of brotherly pride. 'Fortunately she'd already finished her race by the time the dragon appeared,'

'And didn't she do well? Third place! Do tell her we'll arrange a medal ceremony soon. These young flyers are proving to be excellent ambassadors for the sport. Things will only get better once Afra Power and Mike Hill open up the Brighton School. Between them they'll offer our young flyers a first class training. Has Amber considered applying?'

Jamie stiffened at the mention of the school, but replied he didn't think Amber had.

Now the race was over Amber was desperate to get back to London – and away from Dr Braithwaite. She'd told him how she'd seen Isaac make the Silver Flame, thinking this was just the sort of information he wanted. She thought he'd be impressed, instead he said he wanted hard facts and instructions for making the fire, not for her to tell him about a fancy light show. Amber's defence that she didn't understand half the things Isaac went on about, like Latin and dragon eggs, didn't hold much sway either.

'If you are having difficulties finding out from Isaac, make friends with Joanna.'

Dr Braithwaite was finding it hard to contain his temper.

'She doesn't like me,' said Amber sulkily.

'Then make her like you,' snapped Dr Braithwaite impatiently. 'Goodness, the only two fourteen-year-old girls on the same racing circuit, it shouldn't be beyond you.'

I'm fifteen,' retorted Amber.

Dr Braithwaite ignored her reply.

'When's your next race?'

Amber scowled angrily. 'A week on Saturday.'

'So there's your chance. Ask Joanna for tips, admire her racing suit, suggest you have coffee.'

Amber stormed out of the room.

'Fine, I'll do it.'

It was a glorious November day – blue sky, crisp air and a brisk wind. The South Downs were looking spectacular. The trees still wore their autumnal colour and glowed ruby red and fiery gold. From the hilltop, where the race was to start, Joanna looked down to the main spectator stands. The racecourse was seething with people, all anxious to witness her first race of the season. She needed to win to guarantee her place in the New Year Derby, but she wanted to win in style with a fast time – well, faster than Hannibal and Ebony, who were competing in the race before hers.

It hadn't been easy since she'd returned from Blackpool. The WDRF had insisted on questioning her at length about what she had seen in her *mind-blend fight* as they were calling it. She'd forgotten most of it, due to the effect of the silver fire, until they dragged it all up again. Her interrogator wanted to know every little detail, stressing that it was Joanna's duty to assist in their inquiries. She'd come out of the session in tears and exhausted. Besides that, Hannibal and Ebony were back in Brixton, at least until after the next race. They kept themselves to themselves most of the time, but still it created a tension in the caves. At least Isaac was back to normal, talking about getting new eggs in to turn. She wasn't sure if he was still seeing Amber, but wasn't brave enough to ask.

Joanna was making her way over to the flyers' pre-race waiting area when she realised that someone close by was calling her name. Amber Penhaligon was walking straight towards her. What did *she* want?

'Joanna! I'm so nervous. There are so many experienced flyers in my race, I'll probably come last.'

Joanna didn't quite know what to reply, so she said the first thing that came into her head.

'No you won't, Dominic's in your race.'

She turned bright red, annoyed at herself. To her surprise, Amber giggled.

'He's not the best flyer, but definitely the best-looking. Is it true he's your boyfriend? I've read so many different things in magazines.' Joanna couldn't believe what she was hearing.

'No, he's just a good friend,' Joanna smiled weakly. Amber smiled back.

'I have to say I love the way you're doing your hair now. I hope you don't mind, but I've done mine the same.'

Again Joanna found herself left tongue-tied. Was

Amber actually trying to be friends? Luckily she didn't have to say anything more as the announcer was calling flyers for the first race to take their positions.

'That's me,' said Amber. 'See you later.'

Excelsior was rather amused when Joanna told him about the conversation.

'Of course she wants to be friends with you,' said Excelsior.

But Joanna was not so easily convinced.

'She's pretty much ignored me up to now!'

They watched the race together. It was a rather boring affair in an unspectacular time, although Amber won and Joanna had to admit she was a good flyer with potential . . . unlike Dominic, who flew in second to last.

Next up was Hannibal and Ebony. It wasn't so much a race, as an annihilation of their competitors. *Perhaps Hannibal is right*, thought Joanna. *It's certainly easier to beat a rival than a friend.*

'Ebony picked up curling all right,' whispered Excelsior. Joanna saw he was right and anxiously turned to watch the digital stopwatch on the nearest screen. The winning time was close to their own course record.

Then it was Joanna and Excelsior's race. There was a

real sense of anticipation in the air. How would the champions respond?

'Time to spice things up a bit.' Excelsior snorted out a spiral of smoke. 'Bet we can knock three seconds off at least.'

As they settled down to race, Joanna's own senses sharpened. Excelsior was raring to go. His attention was on the wind, sensing its power as it whisked the birds across the sky away to their right.

'Strong cross breeze. And the sun will be in our eyes up to the turn,' he announced.

And then they were off. Excelsior flew out fast on a slow climbing gradient. The spectators below were nothing more than a colourful blur beneath them as they zipped effortlessly ahead. But Joanna and Excelsior were acutely aware that an eagle-eyed Hannibal was watching below, noting every flick of tail, every twist of body, every flap of wing.

The incident happened as they were preparing to 'curl' for a fast finish. Out of the corner of her eye Joanna caught sight of Amber walking towards the finish line. From this distance the logo of the two dragons on her suit was a blurry red and white shape. And with a jolt Joanna realised what it reminded her of – the red and white triangle pattern she had seen on the mystery flyer. For some reason, this sent a chill through her.

177

'JoJo – concentrate!' Excelsior's anxious thoughts pulled her back to the race. 'You were supposed to start the 'curl' two seconds ago.'

It didn't cost them the race, but they lost out to Hannibal and Ebony, who took the trophy for fastest time.

Joanna was furious with herself. 'Sorry, sorry XL – it was all my fault. I was . . .'

'Distracted by Amber's suit?' Excelsior was not impressed.

As the official times went up on the board Joanna suddenly found herself accosted by Dominic and Amber.

'We're off to get a burger and coke,' said Dominic.

Before she could refuse, she found herself being dragged along to a burger van.

'My treat,' said Amber, 'Ketchup?'

Joanna could see Spiky Mike looking around for her.

'Thanks, Amber, but I can't stay. I need to see Spiky Mike – he's not going too pleased that I didn't get fastest time.'

'We'll come and be moral support,' said Amber.

Without waiting for Joanna's reply, they started walking with her back to Spiky Mike.

'I'd rather you didn't.' Joanna pushed Dominic away harder than she had intended and rushed hurriedly past Amber. She didn't stop to apologise, but just ran off. Her head was full of too many things – losing to Hannibal, having to explain her lapse of concentration to her trainer and finally the niggling similarity between Amber's jacket and that mysterious advert she'd seen at Blackpool . . .

24
GIRLS HAVING TOO MANY SECRETS

Joanna swallowed her pride and was more than ready to be generous in her praise of Hannibal's victory. If anything she was rather relieved it was over. She suspected Hannibal's friendly behaviour the next morning was due to his relief at having taken fastest time. She could hardly believe the way he just strolled into Excelsior's cave.

'Hey, Jo. Looking forward to the new Intervarsity race? I know I am – especially after yesterday.' He rubbed his hands in anticipation.

'You flew brilliantly,' said Joanna 'I can see how hard you've been training.'

He stopped smiling, and waited for a second before continuing.

'Look, please don't be upset, but I'm taking Ebony back to train in Brighton. I've got her racing just as I want.' He stopped and dropped his eyes to the floor. 'It is hard for me too, Jo . . .'

Joanna was ashamed to admit to herself that she was relieved at the news. Ebony had made no effort to fit in at the Brixton Caves the previous week. Excelsior claimed she had blanked him every time he had tried to communicate with her.

'So when are you going?'

'Tomorrow.'

Isaac rushed in to the cave.

'Have you heard the news? The WDRF have just issued a statement saying they reckon both dragons washed on the beaches were killed in illegal fight clubs.'

Hannibal shifted uneasily. His first dragon, Prometheus had been more a fighting dragon than a racing dragon and it had nearly cost Hannibal his life.

'Why do people do it?' asked Joanna. 'It's too horrible to think about.'

'For the thrill and excitement – and money. Huge amounts are bet on illegal fights,' replied Hannibal. 'Did the report say what they're doing about it? Poor Mom – she's delayed her trip back to the States twice now. At this rate she'll miss the Thanksgiving Derby in New York.'

'It only says that Interpol and the Serious Organised Crime Agency are working closely together to find out who's behind it.'

They all stood there, not saying anything, till Hannibal changed the subject.

'When are you guys coming down for a visit the school? You should see what Afra and Spiky Mike are doing there. The dragon caves are all refurbished and the new classrooms will be finished by Christmas. You should see the number of applications they've had already.'

'Oh yeah,' said Joanna, frowning. 'The school! Part of me wishes that would just disappear.'

Hannibal frowned. 'Wait till you see it, Jo.' He checked his watch. 'Look I've got to go. Can't be late for lunch with my girlfriend. Niamh says 'hi' by the way. And believe me you'll love the school.'

'I'm sure the school's amazing,' replied Joanna despondently, as Hannibal disappeared out of the cave. 'So amazing that everyone will go down to Brighton, and I'll be left here on my own.'

Isaac laughed. 'Jo, you always forget one vital thing in all of this. Guess why there are so many applications?'

Joanna looked at Isaac blankly. ''Cos flying a dragon is brilliant?'

He shook his head. 'Everyone dreams that they'll be like you – world champion and best friends with a dragon.'

Thanks!' said Joanna. Such a compliment meant a lot to her coming from Isaac.

'Take Amber, she thinks you're amazing. She's so desperate to come and visit. It's all she talks about these days. I was thinking of asking her over.'

Joanna tried to think of something to say. She'd begun to hope Isaac had got over Amber, but obviously she was wrong.

Isaac took her silence for agreement because he said, 'Great, I'll arrange that.'

He hurried out of the cave in high spirits. 'See you tomorrow, Jo. Just need to get the next volume of Magnus Crascus' diaries from Vincent's study, then I'm heading home. Mum's cooked a big Sunday roast and she'll kill me if I'm late.'

Joanna knew she should be getting back too, but instead she asked Excelsior to come down to the indoor flight cave.

'I just need to fly,' was all she had to say.

They took off from the centre of the huge, dark, silent cave and flew round in ever increasing spiralling circles. Soon they were level with the viewing balcony halfway up the cave wall, until finally they were so up high that Joanna could touch the roof of the cave. And that was when they caught sight of a flash of gold, crouched in a small opening where the cave wall met the roof. Hermes! He didn't move, but sat watching them with his bright fiery eyes.

They flew right past him as he sat in the opening of

the air duct. They circled the cave again, but on their return Hermes had gone.

'Fly a bit closer, XL,' said Joanna. 'I want to go and see what Hermes gets up to.'

Excelsior flew close enough for Joanna to slide off his back headfirst into the tunnel.

'I'll wait here,' he said as she disappeared into the darkness.

There was enough room for Joanna to crawl comfortably along on her hands and knees. The surface of the passage way was smooth and flat and there was a strong through draught. It was lucky that the tunnel was dead straight, because the pitch-blackness was disorienting. She was about to turn back when she caught the sound of dragons speaking. Joanna recognised Hermes' high squeaky rasp. And it was followed by a soft hiss – Ebony! She realised she'd hardly ever heard Ebony speak aloud. Curiosity got the better of her and Joanna crawled on.

'JoJo, what are you doing?' She heard Excelsior's thoughts in her mind.

'Ssh, I'll tell you when I get back.'

She felt her way along the wall and, with some trepidation, she took a sharp right into a new tunnel, where she thought the voices were coming from.

I hope I don't get lost in here she thought. The tunnel was short and soon came to an end. It was a T-junction with passages immediately to right and left. The sound of the dragons was coming from the right. Joanna made her way to the end of the tunnel where it turned sharp left. Peering round the corner she could just make out Hermes' dark outline sitting in the opening down to the cave. She could hear him quite clearly now.

'You should tell them, Ebony.'

Ebony's reply was too quiet for Joanna to make out.

Joanna edged forward. What was Ebony saying? She could try listening in a mind-blend but they might know she was there.

'OK, it's your secret, but it seems to me it's making you one unhappy dragon.'

Ebony let out an anguished wail that even Joanna could hear.

'You have no idea!'

Her voice dropped suddenly again so that Joanna could no longer hear her.

'How could there be anyone else up here with me?' exclaimed Hermes loudly.

Ebony could hear *her*? Joanna silently started to move backwards along the tunnel. She had to get out of there before she was discovered. She tried to go quickly, but she didn't dare make a noise. Then a cold wave hit her as she realised that she'd been crawling for so long she must have missed the T-junction that led back the way she'd come in. She had no choice but to go back the way she'd come until she found the junction. She knew she must be getting close because just ahead of her she heard Hermes' claws scratching on the passage floor. She heard him give a low hiss.

'I was so close to finding out her secret and then you came clattering along. ' Hermes sounded really cross.

Joanna was really shocked. 'I was as quiet as a mouse!'

'All your thoughts were spilling out – luckily Excelsior was able to cover up for you.'

'I'm sorry, Hermes. But why all the secrecy? What's up with Ebony?'

'That's what I was trying to find out. Early this morning, I was exploring the ventilation tunnels when I overheard her talking to herself. You must have noticed how sounds carry.'

Joanna nodded.

'She hadn't a clue I was there. She was muttering to herself and crying. Actually crying!'

'Perhaps she'd heard the news about the Dragon Fight Clubs?' suggested Joanna. 'I'm sorry I disturbed you before you could find out.'

Hermes hissed, 'Next time leave it to the dragons. Come on, I'll show you where the next turning is, then all you need to do is crawl to the end the passage.'

Hermes left Joanna once she could see a dim light ahead of her. But when she got to the light she stopped, stunned. There was a thin wire mesh over the opening. That wasn't right. Where was she? Looking down she recognised the room immediately: Vincent's study. Isaac was standing by the fireplace. His eyes were closed and his head bent over in deep concentration. He was running his fingers over the words carved in the stone fireplace. As his fingertips curled round the chiselled shape of each word he spoke it aloud.

ignem amore accende

Isaac stopped for a moment, then started to whisper something . . . she couldn't hear what. He held out his hands towards the fireplace and Joanna saw a tiny silver flame dancing in the grate. He breathed deeply and spoke again, out loud this time. 'Amber.' Instantly the flame died.

Isaac bent down to look in the fireplace.

'Why not Amber?'

If he expected an answer he didn't wait to find out. Instead he snatched up a book from the table, quickly flicked off the small lamp and left the study, slamming the door behind him.

Joanna stared out in to the darkness of Vincent's study. Isaac couldn't make the fire when he thought of Amber! But what did that mean? She felt guilty to have spied on him at such a private moment, but she couldn't supress an unbidden flutter of happiness.

'JOJO!' Excelsior's thoughts suddenly came bursting through. 'Where are you?

Before Joanna could reply, she heard Hermes behind her.

'She's in the ventilation tunnel above Vincent's study spying on Isaac.'

Joanna listened in disbelief. 'You brought me here on purpose.'

'Find out what you wanted to know?' was Hermes' reply.

Joanna glared back at the dragon. 'Can't a girl have any secrets round here?'

'That's just the problem,' sniffed Hermes. 'Girls having too many secrets!'

25
AMBER COMES
TO VISIT

Isaac had started egg-turning again, after Mouse's dad had turned up at the Brixton Caves on the last day in November with a box of five eggs he'd got from a Scottish colleague who could no longer afford to look after them. They were already seven months old and due to hatch the following July. They would have an instant home at the Brighton School.

The evening egg-turning was soon Joanna's favourite part of the day. It had a quiet rhythm all of its own. Joanna would just sit quietly on the bench and watch as Isaac methodically turned one egg after another until she knew his routine perfectly, even the order of lifting out the fireboxes – left to right, high to low. Afterwards he would fill in the egg-turning diary and tell her how the eggs were changing. He never mentioned Amber and she didn't ask.

Then one Friday morning about two weeks later Joanna discovered a clean shirt hanging up in the egg-turning office and a message from Isaac.

See you after school. Amber's coming to watch the egg-turning.

Her heart sank. She hated the thought of Amber at the egg-turning. She couldn't bear to think of her being all friendly and smiley and flicking her hair . . . and Isaac paying her all the attention and ignoring Joanna.

But if Joanna had expected sympathy from Excelsior she was very much mistaken.

'These are your caves! You take charge . . . only don't forget to brush your hair so you can swing it around, and how about some of your shiny lip gloss?'

'Ha ha!' said Joanna, grabbing her school bag. 'How about while I'm studying quadratic equations with Mr Hogan this morning you come up with some amazing master plan to distract Isaac from Ms *Flicky* Hair this evening.'

Joanna decided to be down in the cave with Excelsior for the moment of Amber's arrival. She did briefly wonder about hanging round the trophy cabinet so she could be casually polishing the World Speed record shield, but realised how ridiculous that was. Much better to have Excelsior close by. As the town hall clock struck five, Joanna caught sight of Isaac hurrying out of the library, past the trophy cabinet and through the doors that lead to the lift. Quick as a flash Joanna ran all the way to Excelsior's cave. She pulled out her plait, brushed out her hair and rubbed her lips with lip-gloss.

'OK, XL. Would Mouse approve?'

'I can always singe her hair if you think it will help,' suggested Excelsior brightly. Joanna wasn't quite sure if he was serious or not.

'Hopefully it won't come to that!' said Joanna. She quickly picked up a magazine and sat with her back leaning against Excelsior's side. She hoped it looked casual. Before long she heard voices, chatting and laughing. Joanna looked up puzzled.

'That sounds like Dominic.'

She heard Isaac just outside in the passageway.

'You know where Excelsior's cave is don't you? Why don't you show Amber and I'll just finish feeding Hermes.' There was a quick knock on the door before it burst open.

'Surprise!' Amber came in laughing, followed by Dominic, looking rather apprehensive. 'Look who I brought with me Joanna, aren't you glad?

Joanna stood slowly up. 'Hello Amber, hey Dominic . . . yes . . . um . . . lovely to see you.'

Amber turned to Dominic with a beaming smile.

191

'See, I told you Jo wouldn't mind you coming too.'

Joanna took a sharp quick breath. *Who said Amber could call her 'Jo'!*

Amber, oblivious to Joanna's annoyance, continued. 'Dominic's staying over with us as his nan can't take him to the Intervarsity race tomorrow,' said Amber.

Neither Joanna nor Dominic said anything, so Amber turned back towards the door.

'Hurry up, Isaac! You must have fed that little dragon by now.'

As if on cue Isaac came back. 'All done. So, if everyone's ready, we can go down to the egg-turning cave.'

Amber immediately linked arms with Isaac as he went out of the door.

'I'll follow you in a sec,' called Joanna.

She wanted a few quiet minutes to sound out what Excelsior had made of it all. But even that was denied her when Dominic didn't leave.

'I'll wait for you, Jo. It's ages since I was here.' He walked round the cave smiling broadly. 'Do you remember the first time I was here and you had that big fight with Isaac?'

'Of course,' she replied. Dominic came and stood close to Joanna. She stared in alarm, as he bent forwards – was he going to try and kiss her?

XL, HELP! she thought to her dragon. Excelsior

did the only thing he could think of and opened his wings, knocking Dominic off his feet. Joanna jumped quickly out of the way.

Um . . . Thanks XL, good thinking.

My pleasure, replied Excelsior. Joanna quickly turned back to Dominic, who was sitting rather shell-shocked on the floor.

'Did you stand on Excelsior's foot or something? You should probably go down to the egg-turning cave while I settle him down. Isaac's turning five eggs – can you imagine, five all at once . . .' She was aware she was babbling anything that came into her head now just to distract him.

Dominic stood up rubbing his arm. 'Don't ask if I hurt myself, will you?'

'I can see you're fine,' replied Joanna, realising how rude it sounded, but how else was she going to get rid of him? But Dominic didn't move. He stood there angrily.

'You don't seem very pleased to see me. I thought you *liked* me.'

'I . . . of course I'm pleased to see you Dominic – and of course I like you. I like all my friends. But . . .' She couldn't put it off any longer. She had to tell him how she was feeling.

'Dominic . . .' She took a deep breath. This was harder than she thought. 'I don't *like you* like you.'

Dominic's face went very pale and pinched looking. 'I don't . . .' She started, but he finished off her sentence for her.

'You don't want me for a boyfriend.' He swept his hand through his fringe, pushing his hair out of his eyes. Was he trying to remind her of what she would be missing?

'No.'

Dominic stood there awkwardly, as if waiting for Joanna to say something more. When she said nothing he added, 'But we are still friends though?'

'Of course,' replied Joanna quickly.

'What took you so long?'

Amber was leaning languorously against the cave wall. Her hair gleamed gold in the light of the oil lamps. She was wearing skinny black jeans, a creamy white jumper, black leather jacket and high-heeled boots. *Of course the boys like you*, thought Joanna, feeling smaller and younger than ever. For one brief second did she regret her decision about Dominic?

'Excelsior was in a strange mood. Joanna needed to calm him down,' Dominic said casually.

'A temperamental dragon, is that all? I thought perhaps you and Jo . . .'

Dominic screwed up his face.

'Me and Jo? We're just friends aren't we, Jo? You've been reading too many magazines.'

Jo smiled brightly at Dominic, relieved he was being nice about it all.

Isaac turned briefly to Joanna with a questioning look. She wasn't sure what he was asking, but pretended it was about Excelsior.

'He's fine. Sorry we're late.'

'Isaac was all ready to start without you, but I persuaded him to wait.' said Amber.

'Jo knows only too well that I don't hang around waiting,' said Isaac, putting on the fireproof gloves he used for the egg-turning. 'So if everyone will go and sit down on the bench, I'll start.'

'Don't I get to see a bit closer?'

Amber walked over to look at the five egg-turning boxes, each one slotted into its own opening in the cave wall.

'Sorry Amber, like I told you, I've got to concentrate.'

Amber gave a girly giggle. 'I remember – I don't help, do I?'

Immediately Dominic said, 'Hey, Amber, sit here next to me, I can see really well.'

He made a space beside him. Joanna smiled to herself. Dominic's heart wasn't too badly dented by her rejection then. She sat in her usual place and waited patiently for Isaac to begin.

Next to her Dominic whispered loudly to Amber. 'Did you see the egg-turning lab in the States when you were there?'

'I did.' Amber's whisper was equally loud. 'It was amazing. State of the art and regulated by computer. There was this one egg-turner, he was so sweet, and he spent all his afternoon showing me round.'

Joanna saw Isaac's whole body tense. They were distracting him just as he was about to turn the first egg. She nudged Dominic in the side, but he ignored her and carried on whispering to Amber. Neither of them was paying any attention to the silver egg cradled in the pale blue flame. This was Joanna's favourite egg. It would hatch into a Silver Spiked-Back dragon – Spiky Mike had discovered it shared the same great grandmother as Excelsior. Isaac had told her it had very unusual silver white markings like three small stars.

'Shut up!' hissed Joanna, louder than she meant to. 'Or go and wait outside!'

Isaac snapped shut the lid and put the firebox back in the cave wall. He turned quickly round and stared angrily down at Joanna.

'What are you making that racket for? The others don't know any better, but I wouldn't have expected it of you!'

Joanna flushed red, embarrassed and angry that he should have spoken to her like that in front of the others, especially when she'd been trying to get them to shut up. No point making any further comment. That would only make things worse.

None of them made a sound and Isaac completed the egg turning without further incident.

'And you do that twice a day for another seven months!' commented Amber as Isaac hung up the fireproof gloves. 'Rather you than me! Doesn't it get a bit . . . boring?'

Isaac looked rather crestfallen.

Joanna leapt to his defence.

'But the markings change and then, as the dragon grows, you can feel it moving inside the shell, like a giant jumping bean.'

'Urgh! That's creepy!' Amber screwed her face up in disgust. 'Let's leave egg-turning and go and see something else. OOH I really want to see Vincent's study!'

She beamed smiles excitedly first at Isaac, then at Dominic. Encouraged by her attention Dominic was equally enthusiastic.

'Please, Jo!'

Vincent's study. Joanna's insides flipped over. She turned to Isaac for support, but Isaac was too busy looking at Amber.

'Vincent's study is private,' said Joanna.

'Come on, Jo. You can't keep people out forever,' complained Dominic. 'What better time than when you're with your friends?'

'I'm not keeping people out,' retorted Joanna. 'Isaac and Mr Hogan use the study all the time, but the things inside are valuable and . . . it's a work place not a place for hanging out, isn't it Isaac?'

She turned to him as second time. Surely he understood.

'Perhaps Dominic's right,' said Isaac. 'Come on Jo, it can't hurt just to open the door and let them see.'

Joanna had no choice. She marched quickly out of the cave, without waiting for the others. She was doing her best to ignore the rival smiles of the two boys and as a consequence she missed the look of triumph on Amber's face. When they arrived at the study Joanna opened the door slowly, as if waiting for something to stop her. To her surprise the light was already on. Mr Hogan was sitting at Vincent's desk, concentrating all his attention on adjusting the height of a series of stands supporting a contraption of glass tubes and beakers. He spoke to her without looking up.

'Hello, Joanna, can you just wait a sec, whilst I just sort out this stand . . . There!' He looked up and smiled. 'Sorry, crucial moment. Did you want something?'

Joanna gave Mr Hogan a huge smile. Now she had the perfect excuse to keep everyone out of Vincent's study.

'Sorry, Mr Hogan, I didn't know you were busy. We'll come back another time.'

Joanna turned to where the others were waiting behind her.

'Mr Hogan is busy doing an experiment.'

She was about to close the door when Isaac pushed past her in to the room, inviting the others with him. Joanna followed them in, reluctantly.

'What is it?' said Amber, looking at the desk.

'It's a special method for making *Aqua Regia*,' answered Mr Hogan. He wheeled his chair from around the back of the desk and picked up a small worn brown leather book. The opened page showed a diagram of bottles and tubes, similar to the ones on the desk.

'Can I see?' asked Amber, holding out her hand.

Ever the teacher keen to facilitate learning, Mr Hogan gave the book to Amber, who skimmed her eyes over it and sighed. 'I can't understand any of it.'

'The experiments are all written in Latin,' said Mr Hogan. 'Isaac and I have been translating it.'

'It doesn't look that impressive, but it's really valuable and quite fragile, so be careful,' warned Isaac.

'OOH,' exclaimed Amber. 'It's to do with how you

cured those dragons that had flu.'

'If we'd known then about the clever contraption in this book then our life would have been much easier,' said Mr Hogan, rather pleased to be able to show off his experiment.

Even though Joanna hated Amber and Dominic being there, she was so curious herself that she came right over to the table.

She watched as the steam passed through a long thin glass tube, where it condensed into a fluid and fell drop by drop into a glass beaker. Mr Hogan wheeled his chair back to the experiment where he adjusted the height of one of the test tubes. Immediately the flow of liquid into the beaker increased. He gave a small cheer and they all stood watching in silence, until Amber, obviously bored, said in a loud voice, 'Pizza anyone?'

Joanna was last up the stairs. Up ahead of her she heard Isaac saying he was keen to come along to watch the Intervarsity race.

Pizza with Amber's fan club was suddenly more than Joanna could bear. She slipped off home, knowing they probably wouldn't even notice.

26
UNIVERSITY
CHALLENGE

They had arrived in Christchurch Meadow in Oxford for the pre-Christmas Intervarsity Race. The place was crowded with colourful hospitality tents, one for each of the Oxford colleges. Joanna and Excelsior had been adopted by the students of Magdalen College and as well as wearing her usual racing colours, a large sticker of the college coat of arms now adorned her racing helmet. A huge crowd from the college were already out in support, delighted they had 'won' the world champion in the ballot. Fortunately they hadn't a clue how incredibly nervous she was feeling. She hadn't been this hungry to win a race in ages.

Jo told Isaac he should go and get a good seat – the race was starting in ten minutes and he needed to be able to see both the Oxford and Cambridge screens – the Intervarsity race was a new format, with half the competitors in each city.

'Funny to think of Hannibal flying this same race in Cambridge,' said Joanna. 'You know he's flying for he's dad's old college – King's. I won't know his time till we finish. I'm so nervous. My tummy is nothing but butterflies.'

'I presumed you'd all be racing here,' said Isaac.

'What?' said Joanna, only half-listening as she watched one of her main rivals, Bartek Szeptunowska on Kracow, arrive. The race official immediately cordoned off the entrance, the signal that all competitors had now arrived.

'It never occurred to me that Amber would be in Cambridge.' Isaac uncharacteristically kicked at the line rope of one of the tents. 'I'm stuck here and Dominic gets to hang out with Amber.'

His words stung Joanna so hard that she turned quickly away and walked straight over to where Spiky Mike had just finished registering Excelsior. Fortunately he was busy rubbing liniment into Excelsior's foot and wasn't looking at her.

'Ready?' he said. 'I know you can do it. Don't think about Hannibal. Don't watch the screens . . .'

'. . . and don't watch the clock. Just fly as fast as you can.' Joanna finished off his sentence for him, before adding silently, *and don't make me more nervous than I already am.*

Spiky Mike gave a quick half laugh.

'Told you before, haven't I?'

Joanna went round to the far side of Excelsior before her trainer could notice the tear that had escaped and was making its own solitary journey down her cheek.

Don't think of Amber, and don't think of Isaac thinking about Dominic thinking about Amber, who'll only be thinking of flicking her hair, snorted a voice that always came with a hiss and silver glow.

'Excelsior, stop listening in!' Joanna turned to her dragon, but at least he made her laugh as he tossed his head from side to side in rather a good imitation of Amber.

'Stop letting her get to you,' insisted Excelsior. 'Or at least wait till after the race.'

A fierce-looking official who looked exactly like one of the stone gargoyles on the university buildings arrived to accompany Joanna and Excelsior down to the starting line. Almost immediately they were off, slaloming round ancient stone spires, skirting round the edges of green trim quads and at one point zooming through arched cloisters. It was a high-octane race with sharp bends, sudden fluctuations of height and speed, plus the additional danger of students from rival colleges intent on sabotage.

Isaac watched the race with eyes peeled on both screens. He was rather ashamed of his outburst at

Joanna. He turned his attention to the Cambridge screen. Hannibal was already in the lead, as expected. Then the camera suddenly changed from Hannibal to focus on the other flyers. He could see Amber. She was in third place. She had to fly Diego hard – their bodies and faces looked tense and strained. At the same moment the Oxford screen focused on Joanna. The line of her body seemed to flow into the contours of Excelsior's neck so that they moved as one.

'How does she do it?'

Isaac wasn't aware he'd spoken out loud, but he must have done because Spiky Mike answered immediately.

'Because she does what I tell her, but more than that, because she trusts that dragon completely . . . and he trusts her.'

Isaac turned his attention back to the Cambridge screen, curious now to observe all the other flyers on their dragons. Only Hannibal matched Joanna for speed but even he didn't seem as relaxed. Everyone one else flew *on* their dragons, not *with*.

Excelsior was in his element and his sleek silver body whipped effortlessly around the course. They quickly left the pack jostling for space in the narrow confines of the ancient buildings, knowing the smallest collision would result in time penalties. They flew along the final straight, following the course of the river where students were crammed into the shallow punts or lined the bank, until, with a final burst of speed they landed to wild cheers. But what was their time? And what was Hannibal's? Joanna closed her eyes, not daring to look at the Cambridge screen. She'd caught sight of it as they came into land and seen Hannibal and Ebony about to touch down.

All around Isaac the crowds chanted Joanna's name. Had she won? Spiky Mike hurried over to wait with Joanna. Her anxious face filled the screen. Then came a close-up of Hannibal. But who did Isaac want to win? Unbidden a small voice whispered, *Joanna* and he sensed a silver flame quiver through him. It was only there for a moment and then it was gone again.

Joanna's time flashed up on the screen. 15.3.04.

And then up came Hannibal's. 15.3.04. A dead heat! But what was the red tag flashing on the Cambridge screen? Time penalty! Had Hannibal incurred a time penalty? A slow-motion replay played across Cambridge screen. There it was! At the start of the race Lancelot was flying immediately behind Ebony and the two had brushed on take-off. It was a three-second penalty. Now the crowd went wild. The jubilant Magdalen College students whisked Joanna away to parade her on their shoulders shouting 'CHAMPIONS!' Joanna was enjoying every second of her victory and waved wildly to the crowds. Isaac thought how different this Joanna was to the everyday Joanna he saw at the caves. It was like she was two different people.

No she's not. Can't you see that yet?

Isaac was startled to hear the dragon's thoughts crash into his mind and looked across at Excelsior.

'XL?'

'You heard me,' said the dragon and promptly looked away.

Isaac was taken aback. Excelsior was cross with him, but why? Before he could ask his phone started to buzz. It was a text message from Mr Hogan.

Can't find Liber Elementorum. Have you got it?

Why would Mr Hogan think he had *Liber Elementorum*? It was so valuable that neither of them ever took it out of the study. Mr Hogan had been using it yesterday evening to set up his experiment. It had to be down the side of something, or under a pile of papers.

He sent a quick text back.

No. Let me know when you find it. Brilliant race.

Of all the race celebrations, this was the one Joanna would remember forever. Laughing uncontrollably as she was hastily crowd-surfed over to a new group of students to avoid the officials, anxious for the return of their champion; being draped in college scarfs and a large Brixton flag so that she felt more like an Egyptian mummy than a dragon flyer; or the moment they tossed first their scarves and finally Joanna high into the air.

It took a good half hour before worried officers, muttering about health and safety regulations, finally managed to get Joanna back to the winners' enclosure.

'Thought you were going to be hoisted from some college flag pole,' commented Isaac as Joanna eventually managed to untangle herself from the knot of scarves.

'Sorry about before,' he added. 'I was being grumpy.'

'That's OK,' said Joanna, still flushed and breathless from the celebrations. 'I never thought I'd be grateful for Dominic's dreadful take-off skills. You'd think from past experience Hannibal would have kept clear of him. He'll be furious! But did you see how brilliantly XL flew the chicane of spires and towers? He kept such a straight line and I just concentrated on staying very still in the centre of the mind-blend . . .'

Isaac's phone rang.

'Hang on, Jo . . . it's Amber. Any messages?'

It was like putting a spoonful of sugar in a fizzy drink and turning it flat. Suddenly all the excitement of winning vanished.

Joanna shook her head and forced a smile. 'No, no message.'

She walked over to where Spiky Mike was loading Excelsior into the back of the transporter.

'I might travel in the back with XL,' she said flatly.

'If you prefer, you look exhausted,' said Spiky Mike. 'Go and get changed and we'll be off. Have you got something to eat and drink back there?'

Before long they were cruising back along the motorway to London. Joanna could hear Isaac and Spiky Mike in the front listening to the football results on the radio. She turned her attention back to Excelsior.

'Funny, beating Hannibal seems to be the easy bit,' she whispered softly to her dragon. 'It's Amber who defeats me every time.'

27
ALL I WANT FOR
CHRISTMAS . . .

Julian Penhaligon took a small package wrapped in shiny Christmas paper and handed it to Dr Braithwaite.

'A small Christmas gift from my daughter,' said Julian. 'She's not coming down to Cornwall for Christmas. Lucky thing is off skiing with a friend.'

Marius King turned the present over. On a small sticker in untidy writing were the words:

Hope you like it!
Amber

'Do thank Amber when next you speak to her. How thoughtful of her to think of sending a Christmas gift.'

'You've done so much for all the family, Dr

Braithwaite,' said Julian. 'And I'll be glad of your company this Christmas. Jamie wanted to be down in Tintagel of course, but drew the short straw and is the duty vet during the festivities.' Julian turned to go, before stopping by the door.

'Nearly forgot – this came for you this morning in the post – probably a Christmas card . . .'

When Julian had gone Marius opened both card and present. First the card postmarked San Francisco. It was from Cliff Heywood. Under the printed greeting Heywood had added in a quick scrawl:

Santa's delivering!

Next, he tore open the silvery hologram wrapping of Amber's gift. It was a small book, little more than a desk diary. He carefully fingered the worn leather cover of the book. Tracing the silver embossed flame on the cover he read the words, *Liber Elementorum*. He quickly turned over the pages, looked at the badly drawn sketches of scientific equipment, test-tubes and glass flasks and thin rubber tubing, all labelled in barely legible Latin. Marius King was delighted. Amber's knowledge of Latin and science was probably negligible, but he strongly suspected that, quite by chance, she had hit the jackpot.

Marius stood up and stared from his window. The

estate garden was drab and leafless; the sea beyond flat and grey. But as far as Marius King was concerned, this Christmas all his wishes were coming true.

Jamie Penhaligon was driving to Brighton. With Ebony being a newly imported dragon, he could always think up some excuse to visit her and, therefore, Afra. Today he planned to invite her out to dinner – he'd find some issue concerning Ebony that would require immediate attention – and then be most sympathetic about her team being pipped to the post in the Intervarsity race.

Jamie made good time, but even so by the time he was driving into Brighton the winter afternoon was dark. The streets were crowded with last minute Christmas shoppers and the shops sparkled with glimmering displays. He drove past the Pavilion, softly glowing like a Chinese paper lantern, and turned down a small side street that led to the drive-in entrance of the caves. He let down his window and pushed the buzzer for entry. To his annoyance it was Spiky Mike who answered. What was he doing there?

'It's Dr Penhaligon,' he announced stiffly. 'I've come for the monthly check on Ebony,'

The door swung open and Jamie drove down the circular roadway that led down to the Brighton Caves. Spiky Mike was waiting for him in the car park.

'Afra said you'd be coming this afternoon. She's out Christmas shopping, but Hannibal's with Ebony. I'll take you down.'

'I'm sure I can find my way if you're busy.' Jamie was keen to be rid of Spiky Mike as soon as possible.

'No, I've finished what I was doing, just waiting for Afra to come back.'

Spiky Mike set off down the tunnel, hands in his pocket, and Jamie strongly suspected he was smiling. Afra surely couldn't be serious in wanting to marry him! The man hadn't shaved, his jeans had holes in the knees and there was some obscure indie band blazoned over his sweatshirt. Jamie's silk tie probably cost more than all the garments he was wearing. This tie was emerald green – Afra's favourite colour. Spiky Mike (*Ridiculous name*, thought Jamie, grateful the dragons had never given *him* a nickname) probably didn't have a clue what Afra's favourite colour was!

Spiky Mike pushed open the door.

'Hannibal, Dr Penhaligon's here to see Ebony.'

He stood back to let Jamie through. Ebony, lying at full stretch and drowsing half asleep, was on her feet in an instant, alert, her wings quivering at her side, the silver crest on her head erect. She let out a small blast of smoke as Dr Penhaligon walked towards her and laid his hand on the sleek, black, sinuous neck.

'She's still very agitated then?' Jamie turned to

Hannibal watching anxiously from the side. He ignored Spiky Mike still standing in the doorway.

'She's not so keen on your visits, Dr Penhaligon, too many injections!' admitted Hannibal. 'But that cream you left really sorted out the rash on her under belly. It's the cold she hates – and the grey winter skies.'

'I'll give her a thorough check. With the New Year Derby coming up she needs to be in tip-top condition.'

From the doorway Spiky Mike's phone buzzed.

'That's Joanna and Isaac wanting to be let in.' To Jamie's relief Spiky Mike disappeared.

'They came down to see the work on the school.' Hannibal filled Jamie in. 'Except they then decided a trip to the funfair was also called for.'

Jamie gave a quick acknowledging smile – and began his examination of Ebony. A few moments later he stopped and started to search through his bag. He turned to Hannibal with a small frown on his face

'I've run out of PH tester – that was silly. I've got another box back in the car, I don't want to stop mid examination so If I give you the keys, can you run and get it for me?'

'No problem.' Hannibal took the keys and disappeared out of the cave.

Jamie Penhaligon stepped back and for a good

minute just stared at Ebony. Then he opened his case, took out a large syringe and walked slowly back to the dragon. His hand was trembling now and there were small beads of moisture on his forehead. He took out a tissue and wiped them away.

Neither spoke until finally Jamie whispered.

'Remember, silence, that's all that's required, otherwise . . .' He nodded at the syringe.

Ebony stood motionless, and silent.

'Good,' Jamie slowly ran his finger across Ebony's neck. 'Glad we continue to understand each other.'

A golden flash suddenly exploded from high out of the cave wall, knocking Jamie off his feet. Sprawled with his back on the ground, he found he couldn't move. He was pinned down by razor-sharp dragon claws piercing the soft wool fabric of his suit! A sharp hiss sounded close to his right ear.

'I heard you. Leave her alone.'

A blast of hot air rushed over his face. Instinctively he shut his eyes and turned his head away. He could smell singed fabric and hair.

'Hermes! Get off!'

Jamie heard the shock and alarm in Hannibal's voice as he rushed forward to rescue Jamie from the wayward dragon. Hermes released his prisoner and in an instant flew up to the air vent in the corner of the cave and disappeared.

Jamie staggered to his feet, his legs shaking uncontrollably.

'I was attacked, out of nowhere!' His voice sound fearful and angry.

'Dr Penhaligon, are you OK? Sit down. Let me call for help.'

Hannibal went over and pressed a red emergency button. Spiky Mike quickly appeared. He looked in shocked surprise at a dishevelled Jamie. 'What on earth has happened?'

'You need to keep that dragon locked up. It's dangerous . . . It just attacked me.'

Jamie couldn't keep the shake out of his voice.

'Ebony attacked you?' Spiky Mike looked incredulous.

'Not Ebony,' snapped Jamie, before Hannibal could answer. 'That gold one.'

'Hermes? What was he doing here?'

'I don't know, do I? The vicious little snake appeared from nowhere and attacked me. And now he's slithered off!'

Spiky Mike turned to Hannibal.

'Get Isaac and Jo to help you find Hermes. Put him in a travel cage in the transporter van while I sort out Jamie.'

Jamie turned on Spiky Mike. 'You're sending teenagers to round up a dangerous dragon! Are you out of your mind?'

Spiky Mike stood his ground.

'I very much doubt that Hermes has suddenly turned dangerous. I don't know why he attacked you, but he must have felt threatened. I think they'll be quite safe. Looks like the only serious casualty is your suit. Sorry about that. Do please bill the caves for a replacement. There's a first aid kit in the office; let's go and sort you out.'

Jamie fingered the ripped fabric of his jacket as he followed Spiky Mike. Was Spiky Mike smiling again?

Fortunately the injuries were little more than minor scratches and Jamie's hair was only slightly singed on top. Far more serious was Jamie's foul mood. He insisted on phoning through a formal complaint that obliged him to take Hermes in for assessment.

Now he knew he wasn't seriously hurt Jamie was rather enjoying turning the tables on Spiky Mike. 'And with it being the Christmas and New Year break, I'm afraid this will take longer than I'd like, but I'm sure you understand.'

'Oh, I understand,' repeated Spiky Mike. He knew full well that Jamie was enjoying this. Before he said anything unwise, he left to see whether the others had caught Hermes . . .

Alone in the office Jamie took out his phone, and opened up the memo pad app. He wanted to record as many details of the incident as he could whilst it was fresh in his memory. He'd make Spiky Mike pay dearly for his cavalier attitude towards safety. He was putting the finishing touches to his memo when Afra arrived laden with Christmas shopping.

'Sorry I'm late, Mike . . .' She stopped on seeing Jamie sitting there. 'Jamie! Your face – it's all scratched and what are those rips in your suit?'

Jamie was delighted to be able to tell his version of the story, but before Afra had chance to be as sympathetic as Jamie would have liked, Spiky Mike returned. For once even he looked uncomfortable.

'Not sure how to tell you this, Jamie, but we can't find Hermes.'

Afra looked questioningly at Spiky Mike, but Jamie slammed down his hand on the table.

'I don't believe you. You have been unhelpful at every turn.'

Spiky Mike came and squared up to Jamie. 'Are you accusing me of lying?'

For a moment Jamie didn't reply. Then it was his turn to smile – a mean thin smile.

'Perhaps you'd prefer the WDRF to send down an emergency squad to search the premises?'

'Jamie!' Afra's voice was shaking. 'I'm sure that won't be necessary.'

'Sorry, Afra. I'm not leaving without that dragon.'

Afra turned to Spiky Mike. 'What about the

ventilation shafts, you know how he loves to explore those?'

'We've searched thoroughly. He must have found some way out of the caves. He's not here.'

Jamie was not to be placated. 'I still want the caves searched.'

'Fine,' said Spiky Mike, 'but I need to get Joanna and Isaac back to London this evening. Isaac has a deadline of 7.30 for the egg turning.'

'As long as Afra is prepared to keep the premises open during the search then you can go.' Jamie tried hard not to show just how pleased he was by this development. 'And I must check your van before you leave.'

'What, in case we smuggle Hermes out with us?' scoffed Spiky Mike angrily. 'Don't mind if I get my things do you? Or do you want to check my briefcase in case Hermes is hiding in there?'

Afra quickly suggested that she took Jamie to check the van whilst Spiky Mike sorted what he needed to take back to London and quickly hurried Jamie out of the office and down to the transporter van. As she opened up the doors Jamie caught sight of Afra's engagement ring which she didn't usually wear for work: emerald. He wasn't sure he'd hated Spiky Mike more than at that moment.

28
MADCAP
THEORIES

When Isaac arrived to feed Excelsior next morning he was surprised to find Joanna already there.

'Bright and early even on Christmas Eve! I thought you weren't training till later?'

'I wanted to give you your present and then I need to talk you . . . about Hermes and Ebony.'

Joanna hesitated. She'd been awake half the night trying to work out what to say, not knowing what Isaac would make of it all. He'd been in such a funny mood as they'd driven back up to London, especially after Joanna had confessed that she was responsible for letting Hermes escape through a safety exit. He'd actually suggested that it would have been better for Jamie to take him. But only because he didn't know all the facts yet. When she told him what Hermes had told her then surely he'd change his mind and be on her side – as deep in her heart she knew he was, wasn't he?

Joanna watched nervously as Isaac carefully unwrapped her present. It was a chain from which hung a tiny silver dragon sitting in the middle of a flame.

'I got one for Mouse too, only hers is a mouse,' said Joanna quickly. 'I wanted something really special for my *best* friends,' she smiled.

For a moment he just stared at the gift.

'It's beautiful,' he said quietly, putting it back in the box. 'Afraid mine's a bit more every day.'

He watched Joanna unwrap a new Latin dictionary for herself and a bottle of wing liniment for Excelsior, before asking, 'OK, so what did you want to tell me about Ebony and Hermes?'

Joanna started by confessing she was very surprised and seriously worried that Hermes hadn't returned to Brixton. Isaac's comment was not encouraging. 'You should have thought about that before you let him go.'

'Don't you want to know why he attacked Jamie in Ebony's cave?' she asked, dismayed.

Excelsior snorted loudly behind her.

'Tell him what Hermes told you before you let him go.'

Isaac looked at Joanna dubiously. 'Go on Jo, tell me.'

'Hermes told me Jamie threatened Ebony, told her to keep silent and he had a large syringe in his hands . . .'

Isaac actually laughed out loud. 'Jo! Jamie's a vet – he gives injections all the time.'

'Except . . .' Joanna desperately wanted to tell Isaac about Jamie sedating the fighting dragon. Tell him how Hermes had discovered Ebony crying. But it was pointless. He had made it very obvious he didn't believe a word she was saying.

'Tell him about the lost book,' Excelsior nudged Joanna. She shook her head.

'What?' Isaac looked from one to the other. 'Go on, let's hear it.'

'*Liber Elementorum* – the book Mr Hogan's lost; the last person to have it was . . . Amber,' said Excelsior before Joanna could stop him. She refused to look up at Isaac but she heard his scornful laugh.

'Amber was looking at the book in the study, so what? We were all there – including you, Jo!'

Excelsior leapt to his flyer's defence. 'So where is it then?'

'I don't know, but I think you both need stop leaping to wild conclusions about the Penhaligons. And accusing Amber! I thought she was your friend!' Isaac's look of disgust made Joanna's cheeks burn red. What if she was wrong?

'I . . .' she started to reply.

'What?' snapped Isaac. 'Need to apologise?'

Joanna didn't reply.

'I don't think I want your present at the moment,' said Isaac, handing back the silver charm. Excelsior snorted loudly and let out a blast of fire.

'And don't lose your temper with me either XL,' Isaac snapped back. 'I'm going. I've got jobs to do.'

He slammed the door behind him leaving a shocked Joanna staring after him. Never mind his Christmas present – it was their friendship he'd just thrown back at her.

29
SHOW
DOWN

The racetrack for the New Year Derby was a cauldron of excitement. Despite the grey skies and cold drizzle, record crowds had come to witness the showdown between Excelsior and Ebony. Large screens reported a constant flow of statistics about dragons and flyers, as well as pre-recorded interviews with Spiky Mike and Afra.

Hannibal's fan club was out in force and had taken over one of the largest stands, draping it with memorabilia, posters, and banners. They had changed the words to an old song and were now singing,

He flies through the air with the greatest of ease that daring young man on E-bo-ny.

Joanna was finding it hard to concentrate on the race. There was still neither sight nor sound of Hermes. He'd been gone over a week. She could only hope he had been taken in by some kind dragon owner for the Christmas break. She'd spent the whole of Christmas wondering how much Ebony knew about Jamie Penhaligon's involvement with the dragon fights. She must have kept her knowledge deeply hidden for Hannibal not to have discovered it in his mind-blend. Joanna was determined to tackle Ebony – force it from her, if necessary. She would go to Ebony's trailer after the race.

Isaac had been deliberately avoiding her since Christmas. He'd come to watch the race and made it very clear that it was Hannibal he would be supporting. As far as she knew *Liber Elementorum* hadn't turned up, even though Mr Hogan and Isaac had been through Vincent's study with a fine toothcomb looking for it.

She changed quickly and made her way out to the pre-race enclosure, past the food kiosks and hospitality tents, where spectators were making the most of the warmth, food and drink prior to the race. Excelsior was waiting for her.

'I've been keeping an eye on Ebony.' His voice was quiet. 'She's put a full mind-block up.'

Joanna nodded.

It was only when the siren sounded, announcing that flyers and dragons should make their way to the start, that it dawned on Joanna they had a race to win. A twist of excitement curled around her tummy as she walked alongside her silver dragon. She heard the announcer say her name, almost drowned out by the cheering of spectators.

With such low cloud they'd be reliant on watching the race on the screens. The soft, wet, misty drizzle was slowly turning to steady rain, making things miserable for the spectators. Ebony hated the rain too. Most dragons did. Surely that must favour Excelsior. Training up in Snowdonia had inured the pair to even the heaviest downpours.

They took off in a sudden deluge. Each beat of dragon wing sent out a spray of water. Clouds of steam swirled from dragon nostrils. They were in blind flight, trusting to sound, vibration and pure speed to avoid fellow competitors. Excelsior was gathering speed now as Joanna deepened the mind-blend, allowing their thoughts to synchronise. From deep within Excelsior's belly she felt the fireball whipping itself tighter like a coiled spring. The fire was hot and bright – like a moth she felt its pull. She didn't hesitate or flinch, but allowed the flames to swallow her up. Deeper and faster, like a champion surfer she rode the wall of fire. She sensed rather than saw Ebony away to their left – nothing more than a dark shadow of dragon rippling through the clouds.

Out of nowhere a flash of angry gold and a stream of red fire cut across them. Excelsior pulled abruptly to the right narrowly avoiding a wayward dragon. Ebony and Hannibal weren't so fortunate and the dragon caught them hard in the side. Hannibal was jolted so heavily that he started to slip off Ebony's back. The crowd gasped – first in horror and then relief as somehow he pulled himself back up. Immediately the emergency siren sounded – the race was being stopped. All dragons were to return to the pre-race enclosure immediately.

Excelsior ignored the siren. He said only one word. 'Hermes.'

The silver dragon swiftly turned back the way they had come. 'Look, JoJo, He's over there by that clump of trees.'

Excelsior landed close by and Joanna ran to his side. The golden dragon was in a pitiful state. His eyes were rolling wildly in his head, his breath erratic – a mixture of red fire and dark grey smoke. His body was trembling and covered in sweat. The dragon was growing more agitated by the second.

'STEP BACK FROM THE DRAGON,' ordered a loud hailer from behind them.

Joanna turned to face the WDRF official. She shuddered to see a group of marksmen all with large stun guns.

'He's not dangerous!' she shouted hurriedly. Oh

poor Hermes. Where had he been? What was he doing at the race?

'MS MORRIS, STAND AWAY.'

'I need to speak to him,' she pleaded, squatting down besides Hermes. Hermes lifted up his head towards Joanna and tried to stagger to his feet. He opened his mouth and something dropped to the ground. Joanna's heart thumped wildly in her chest as she picked up a crumpled piece of paper. She recognised it immediately – the advert with the strange triangular pattern that reminded her of the dragons on Amber's jacket.

Zap! A sedative dart whistled past Joanna and planted itself in the dragon's back flank. Instantly, Hermes keeled over, unconscious. The official ran forward and pulled Joanna away from the inert dragon.

'You're quite safe now, Ms Morris.' Joanna turned angrily on the official.

'Safe? I was never in any danger. What are you going to do with Hermes now?'

The man looked startled. 'You know this dragon?'

'Of course,' snapped Joanna. 'He's a dragon from the Brixton Caves. I'd like it if you could call Spiky Mike so that we can arrange to take Hermes home.'

To be fair to him, the official did phone to ask for further clarification, but, as Joanna feared, Hermes was to be taken into WDRF custody.

227

Joanna stormed back to Excelsior. 'I'm going to ask Ebony right now what's going on.'

Excelsior did not need to be told twice. He flew back to the enclosure where all the contestants were milling about waiting for further news. Ebony was surrounded by officials as well as Hannibal and Afra, but Joanna pushed her way through and before Ebony had chance to realise what she was doing Joanna had taken control of a mind-blend.

'What's going on? You tell me now.' Joanna held the dragon's mind tight within her own. Ebony resisted, by protecting her thoughts in a wall of fire. Joanna started to force her way through the fire, but a strong pair of arms dragged her away from the dragon, forcing Joanna to break the mind-blend. It was Spiky Mike. He looked as white as a sheet. Joanna wriggled out of his grasp and ran over to Excelsior. He roared a torrent of fire into the air as a warning shot if any WDRF officials tried to intervene. Joanna pointed grimly at Ebony.

'Ask her. Someone demand to know what she's keeping secret!'

Ignoring Excelsior, Spiky Mike walked straight over to Joanna.

'Whatever the problem is, I believe you. But this is not the way to solve it. I want you to take Excelsior over to the dragon transporter now.'

'But Hermes . . .'

'Hermes is safe, and will answer fully when he is awake.'

'But . . .'

'Jo!' Spiky Mike looked straight at her. 'Do as I say and I stand by you. Disobey and Excelsior will find himself in a similar position to Hermes and things will be beyond my control.'

'Do as he says, XL,' muttered Joanna, all the fight suddenly gone out of her.

She saw Spiky Mike breathe out slowly. He turned and nodded to Afra, who was standing in front of Hannibal to stop him from coming over to Joanna.

'I'm sorry . . .' she mouthed as walked passed him. He looked away, but not before Joanna had seen the look of accusation and betrayal he gave her. Joanna felt sick to her stomach. Hannibal had every right to be furious with her. She knew how angry she'd have been if Hannibal had tried to mind-blend with Excelsior . . . but what other option had she had?

She sat in the front of the transporter van staring out of the window waiting for Spiky Mike, who was a few metres away, talking with Afra. Joanna saw Jamie Penhaligon approaching. As soon as he reached the couple, Spiky Mike and Jamie began to argue about Hermes.

Joanna was distracted from the argument briefly by

Amber and Isaac passing by with Diego. They walked right past the van without looking up. Perhaps they didn't see her through the misted-up windows. Or perhaps they deliberately didn't try.

She could hear them laughing and joking as they loaded up Diego into Jamie's transporter van and felt more alone than ever. She wished Mouse had come down to watch the race. Soon they were finished and Joanna saw them heading to a hot-dog stand. She wiped a hole in the misted glass and watched as Jamie Penhaligon loaded Hermes. At least the golden dragon would have Diego for company if he woke up. Poor Hermes. But why hadn't he gone home to Brixton? Why come to the racecourse?

She took the flyer from her pocket and smoothed it out. He was trying to tell her something. Something important enough that he would risk being caught.

If Mouse was correct about the top numbers, *something* was happening at seven o'clock this evening. But what did the bottom numbers mean?

Joanna was still racking her brains when the door to her own van opened and Spiky Mike climbed in.

'Penhaligon is demanding that Hermes is taken into WDRF custody for the time being so that his mental state can be assessed. He's also insisting that Afra and Hannibal bring in Ebony to have her checked over. Hermes rammed straight into Ebony's side and internal bruising is a real possibility. They're all driving over to Wimbledon. Isaac's going back with them. I'll drop you and XL in Brixton, and then head on to join them I don't like leaving Hermes like this.'

Even as he spoke, Joanna saw Jamie's juggernaut pull out, followed by Afra driving Ebony's van.

Spiky Mike started the engine. But instead of pulling away down the road, the van spluttered to a halt and there was a nasty smell of burning. The day was going from bad to worse.

Spiky Mike rang for a mechanic, but on New Year's Day it was going to be a long wait.

The real problem was Excelsior. No recovery vehicle would agree to tow a van with a dragon onboard. Joanna and Spiky Mike were sitting in the clubhouse discussing their options when Julian Penhaligon came over to their table.

He nodded amiably at Spiky Mike and Joanna.

'I couldn't help overhearing your transport problems. Can I be of any assistance? I have one empty dragon transporter van as Amber has ditched me in favour of her brother's shiny juggernaut. I can easily drop you at the Brixton Caves, that's Lambeth Town Hall isn't it?'

Spiky Mike jumped up and shook Julian by the hand enthusiastically. 'That's more than kind of you, Julian. I'll just make a quick call to the garage and ask them to pick up our van in the morning.'

'It's not the most glamorous of transporters,' said Julian apologetically. 'But despite Amber's protests that I drive far too slowly, I should have you home about seven.'

They were soon packed up and on the way. It was warm in the front, sandwiched between Julian and Spiky Mike, and Joanna was soon feeling quite sleepy. She woke up with a jolt as Julian braked hard to avoid an impatient motorbike jumping the lights. An untidy pile of papers precariously balanced on the dashboard tumbled on to Joanna's lap.

'Just drop them on the floor and I'll sort them out later,' said Julian. 'There could have been a nasty accident. I'm just going to stop and check Excelsior didn't take a knock.'

As Joanna dropped the pile of papers on to the floor she saw a brochure for the Tintagel Caves. Emblazoned across the top was a shield showing the Penhaligon coat of arms.

She picked it up. There was that shape again of two opposite triangles of red and white.

She took out Hermes' flyer. Glancing over, Spiky Mike said, 'I kept seeing adverts like that today at the racecourse.'

'Do you know what it's for?' asked Joanna. 'Hermes was carrying this one in his mouth. I think the top numbers are time and date, but I can't work out what the bottom ones are.' She handed the crumpled flyer to her trainer.

'It's a grid reference,' he said straightaway. 'Look it up on your phone.'

Julian Penhaligon climbed back up into the cabin of the van. 'Excelsior's fine. Nearly back anyway.'

Joanna let Spiky Mike do the listening to Julian's

plans about developing the Tintagel Caves, while she tried to work out the grid reference. She thought she must be doing something wrong, because it kept coming up with Lambeth Town Hall. She must have some GPS homing device turned on.

'Here we are, perfect timing,' said Julian with a smile, turning into the loading bay of the Brixton Caves. 'Seven o'clock exactly!'

30
THE
TRUTH

Isaac leant against the window of the giant transporter and watched the world speeding past. He briefly glanced down to read a text message from Joanna. Could he pass on a message to Jamie – they'd broken down but Julian Penhaligon was giving them a lift back to Brixton and Spiky Mike would get over to Wimbledon as soon as he could. Seconds later came a second message telling him she desperately needed to speak to him as soon as possible to explain everything.

He didn't reply to either text. Joanna had nothing to say to him that could excuse her behaviour. Perhaps the rumourmongers were right and she was having some sort of breakdown. OK, she'd always been highly-strung and emotional – and ready to fly off the handle if she didn't like something – but she hadn't really been right since winning the World

Championship. The list was endless – mistaking the doping test vet for Marius King, fainting left right and centre, ridiculous accusations against Jamie and Amber and now, today, forcing Ebony into a mind-blend . . . Amber was so different. She just wanted to have fun, to hang out with friends – and no conspiracy theories! Isaac was glad to see her without Dominic, who was still away skiing, not having qualified for the New Year Derby. Sitting beside him, in the middle passenger seat, she was plugged into her phone, listening to music and mouthing the words.

She took out her earphones. 'Do you fancy some Chinese when we get to Wimbledon? I could phone through now. I think I've got a menu at the bottom of my bag.'

Amber scrabbled around in her bag, pulling out a comb, lip-gloss, keys, taxi cards and other bits of pieces.

'I think it's one of these,' she said handing Isaac a handful of paper. 'Have a look whilst I put all my stuff back.'

'Don't leave any of your rubbish on the floor either,' snapped her brother crossly. 'My van is not your wastepaper bin.'

'I won't order you any Chow Mein if you're going to be cross,' said Amber spiritedly.

'Here's that advert again,' said Isaac; going through the pile Amber had given him. 'I saw these all over

Blackpool and there were a whole load of them fly-posted today. Do you know what they're for?'

Amber tried to snatch it from him. 'Someone gave it me today, I just bunged it in my bag.'

Isaac persisted. 'It's got today's date, but I still don't know what the bottom code is for.'

'Who cares?' said Amber, trying for a second time to get the flyer.

'Can I see?' said Jamie, suddenly pulling over to the side of the road. Amber handed him the advert. Jamie looked at the advert and threw it down. He sat there with his head in his hands muttering to himself, 'Not again! You promised you wouldn't get involved again.'

'What is it Jamie?' Amber had turned deadly pale.

'Do you know what that advert means?' asked Isaac with growing concern.

'The numbers are a grid reference number for a map,' said Jamie flatly.

Isaac took out his phone.

'What are you doing?' Amber asked sharply.

'Looking it up, of course.' He fiddled with his phone for a couple of seconds. 'But that's Lambeth Town Hall.'

Amber snatched the phone out of his hands and turned to her brother. 'But you've got to stop it.'

Jamie took his sister firmly by the shoulders. 'What makes you think I can stop it?'

'I know you run the fight clubs . . . with Dr Braithwaite . . .' she gulped. 'I overheard you at Tintagel . . . I saw the fight.'

Isaac sat there listening in horror. *Fight club?*

Jamie's voice shook as he spoke to his sister. 'I'm not running any fight club.'

'Liar,' she shrieked. 'I heard you in the cave down by the beach arranging it all with Dr Braithwaite.'

Jamie shook his head. 'Dr Braithwaite's Dad's friend not mine.'

Amber wiped her mottled and tear-stained face with her hand. 'Dad?' She stared up at her brother, confused. 'But Dr Braithwaite said . . .' She stopped. Dr Braithwaite had never actually said her brother was involved – she'd jumped to that conclusion.

Isaac pulled Amber round to face him, ignoring her tears. He felt sick to the pit of his stomach as he remembered Joanna's text about getting a lift from Julian Penhaligon.

'Does this mean there's a fight club at the Brixton Caves tonight?'

She nodded.

There was a sudden knock at the cab door. Isaac saw Hannibal and Afra looking up questioningly.

Isaac pulled open the door handle and almost fell out of the cab of the transporter.

'Is there a problem?' asked Hannibal. 'Why have you pulled over?'

Isaac held out the advert. 'Julian Penhaligon and Dr Braithwaite have arranged a fight club tonight in the Brixton Caves.'

Afra let out a cry and started to run back to her van, but Jamie jumped down out of the cab and tried to stop her.

'Where do you think you're going?'

She pulled away. 'To Brixton, of course. Mike will be there '

'Afra please, don't go. It's too dangerous. I couldn't bear it if any thing happened to you.'

Afra turned to him coldly.

'If you think I would wait here whilst the man I love is in danger then you don't know me, Dr Penhaligon.'

'And I'm coming too,' said Isaac. He turned to Hannibal. 'Take me on Ebony. It will be quicker.'

Hannibal nodded.

'Don't be fools!' shouted Jamie. 'Afra, there's nothing you can do.'

She turned back to Jamie. 'I'm taking Hermes too. I don't trust the Penhaligons anymore.'

'I had nothing to do with the Fight Club,' said Jamie weakly. 'All I ever did was look after the injured dragons.'

'Just get Hermes,' snapped Afra.

Isaac climbed up behind Hannibal on to Ebony's back. Amber shouted something, but he didn't hear and really he didn't want to know. All he could think of were his friends in danger. Ebony was fast, but would she be fast enough to make any difference? As they took off into the air, Isaac suddenly realise they had a travelling companion – Hermes.

31
GRAND
FINALE

Excelsior was awake. He was lying in his own cave. But he didn't know how he had got there.

'JoJo?' He called out, knowing she wasn't there. He tried to get to his feet and found he could barely stand. He slithered back down to the ground and closed his eyes again. Something was badly wrong. His head was aching and the fire in his belly felt weak and sluggish. He heard a voice he recognised calling to him from the doorway. It sounded like Julian Penhaligon.

'Wake up dragon. The sedative wasn't that strong. People are waiting and they're growing impatient.'

Excelsior's eyes snapped open this time and dragged himself up to his full height.

'Where is JoJo? If you have hurt her . . .'

'Now why would you think I have hurt her? Joanna

is waiting for you by the indoor arena. She's talking to an old friend.'

Excelsior was about to send a blast of fire out in Julian Penhaligon's direction when he noticed another figure beside him. Spiky Mike! He'd obviously been sedated too and was only just coming round.

'A little insurance policy,' said Julian, 'to make sure you behave. Although, if I were you, I'd save your fire, dragon. You're going to need it. Let's go and find Joanna, shall we?'

Excelsior gave a low growl of displeasure and walked out of the cave.

Joanna was standing outside the huge wooden doors of the indoor arena. Her hands were tied behind her back and there was a rope around her neck. If she moved she'd choke, so she stood as still as she could.

She had imagined this moment too many times, but now that it was really happening it was a million times worse. Even with his slimmer figure, new nose, dyed hair and tinted heavy rimmed glasses she'd recognised him straightaway. Marius King. Come to get her, as she always knew he would. If only she knew what had he done to Excelsior and where Spiky Mike was. The last time she'd seen either of them had been when Spiky Mike had gone to get Excelsior out of the van – just before someone had come and placed a thick sack over her head and dragged her to the lift.

'What do you want?' she managed to ask. Her throat was too dry. She could feel her heart thumping too hard. But she would not cry in front of this man.

'What do you think?' He laughed a thin cruel laugh. 'At long last it's time for the *Grand Finale*. It's all very exciting – I've been planning it for months – Cornwall, Blackpool and now Brixton. The most extraordinary thing is how close by you've been all along. I like to think that somehow you have co-operated and made it happen. And we have an audience! So many people were disappointed today not to see the derby. But this is so much more exciting than any race. Let me introduce you.'

He pushed open the doors and dragged her into the centre of the huge indoor arena where the large floodlights were burning full blaze.

'Take a good look. See how many people you recognise.'

The balcony, set up high in the left cave wall, was a sea of faces. It came as a terrible shock to recognise her parents and her brother. And there was Agnes and Mr Hogan. Sitting behind them Joanna recognised various race officials and trainers, even the ex-President Sir John Miller. On seeing Joanna they all started yelling and screaming in protest.

Marius King waved magnanimously up to the balcony and turned to Joanna with a twisted smile.

'A very select audience to watch the event 'live', but it's also being relayed around the world.'

A giant screen, high up on the wall, suddenly flashed into life. Joanna looked up to see her own pale face staring back at her.

Marius King tugged the rope holding Joanna captive, dragging her over to the cave wall. A hook had been roughly hammered into the rock face. Marius King threaded the rope through the hook and tied it off in a knot.

'Wouldn't want you running off now,' he laughed. He ignored her cries and turned his attention back to the balcony. 'Ladies and gentlemen, take your seats. The show is about to begin!'

Joanna was vaguely aware that Julian Penhaligon was hurrying up the balcony stairs. He stopped on the top stair and stood there, clearly guarding the balcony door from any would-be escapees. Slumped at the bottom of the stairs was Spiky Mike. He raised his hand weakly in Joanna's direction, before it flopped back on to his lap.

Marius King's voice boomed out from the speakers.

'Tonight we say farewell to dragon racing as we know it and embrace in its place a new sport – the dragon fight club.'

He ignored the screams and cries that erupted from the balcony.

'And what better contestant could there be than our world-racing champion, Excelsior, in his own Brixton Caves.'

Joanna glimpsed a flash of silver crouched on the ground, just in front of the cave doors and turned slowly to look, full of dread at what she knew she would see.

Excelsior looked so small . . . so small and bright and skinny compared to the roar that seemed to be filling up all the space in the cave.

Joanna could only stand there, stunned. Above the hammering of her heart, above the frantic shouts from the balcony above, above Marius King's manic laugh echoing off the cave walls was a dark violent roar, relentless like the boom of waves pounding rocks, like the deepest rumble of thunder.

'This is it – your Grand Finale' announced Marius King, as he casually strolled the long length of the indoor arena, and threw open wide the doors that led to Ebony's Cave.

'Behold, Armageddon!'

32
ARMAGEDDON

A foul stench of sulphurous yellow smoke erupted from the cave opening. Within, there was slow movement, a body uncoiling, lengthening, widening to reveal a shimmer of deep emerald green. It slithered forward out of the darkness. In an instant it raised itself on to muscular back legs, revealing a belly encrusted in dazzling firestones that flashed ruby, sapphire and topaz. Its sinuous neck snaked hypnotically to right and left; the stare from its slit of red eyes was greedy and malicious. Flames and twisting smoke spewed out from nostrils and mouth, whilst along its back razor-sharp spines were raised ready for attack.

'A Jewel dragon. My God, that's a *fighting* Jewel dragon.' Spiky Mike had staggered to his feet to try and reach Joanna.

'Stay where you are,' hissed Marius King.

Armageddon sent out a spray of fire as if in warning. Spiky Mike hastily sat back down. The Jewel dragon watched for one brief moment as if enjoying his little game before turning slowly to face Excelsior. The silver dragon was rooted to the spot, transfixed by fear. Crouching low to the ground, each muscle taut and tense, Armageddon splayed out his claws ready for the attack. He struck!

With a cry of anguish Excelsior leapt into the air, his only hope lay in his speed and agility. But for how long could he avoid the relentless attack from such a beast? Immediately Armageddon was in close pursuit. Each beat of wing bringing him closer to his target. The spectators screamed in horror at their close-up balcony view. To Joanna, Excelsior looked little more than a grey shadow.

'We've got to help him,' Joanna mouthed pleadingly to Spiky Mike, but he just stared back at her, dazed and helpless.

She was on her own and she couldn't move. There was only one option. She had to mind-blend with Armageddon and take control of him. She turned all her attention on the monstrous beast.

What are you? She demanded, forcing her thoughts into the dragon's mind. Armageddon stopped in mid-air for one brief second as he replied,

I am a dragon
What is your name?

Joanna could feel the pull of his angry twisting red fire dragging her down into his thoughts. She had to stay in control . . .

Waves of contempt and hatred were flowing through her, burning her up.

Die! Death! Kill! Kill! Kill!

She was shrieking now; open to the roar that was growing all around her.

With one huge effort she wrenched her thoughts away.

He was too strong.

She had failed.

Nobody down in the street below noticed the sleek black dragon land on the roof of the town hall, bypassing the police cordon outside the town hall. But the flight had been the easy part. Hannibal and Isaac were now faced with how they would access the caves. It was Hermes who reminded them about the ventilation tunnels. Hermes removed a small grid, revealing a dark entranceway. Hannibal shook his head. He didn't stand a chance of squeezing into such a tiny space. Suddenly they realised they had been spotted. Up above them a police helicopter caught them in a beam of light and a voice over a loud hailer was calling to them to get down off the roof. It was now or never. Isaac stared in horror at the small black vertical opening. Was there now other way?

'Joanna has been in the ventilation tunnels,' said Hermes and flew inside. Isaac nodded. If Joanna could do it then he could too. He sat down on the edge of the opening of the tunnel. There was a small metal ladder running down the shaft. His feet found the rungs and he followed Hermes down into the darkness, hoping and praying that the ladder would hold.

Facing those narrow tunnels in the pitch black was the scariest thing he'd ever done. But it faded to insignificance when it came facing the truth of the thoughts running through his mind.

This is my fault. I chose not to believe Jo because . . . Because he'd thought Amber was glamorous and stylish . . . and he'd been flattered that she'd noticed him.

He gave a little bitter laugh. It was obvious now. Amber didn't care for anyone but herself, whereas Jo . . . He knew he'd let her down badly. Treated her like some irritating kid sister. She'd never given up on him, though, not even when he'd failed so miserably in making the silver fire for Hermes' egg. In that moment, in the darkness of the ventilation tunnels, it dawned on Isaac that Joanna more than just liked him. The chain for Christmas had been her way of telling him how she'd felt and like an idiot he'd thrown it back in her face. Why now, when it was too late, did he realise just how much he cared for her?

Hermes, who was leading the way, suddenly stopped.

'Listen,' he said. 'The fight has begun. We need to hurry.'

Isaac chased after Hermes as the gold dragon sped along the tunnels, the roars and cries growing stronger and louder all the time, until suddenly Isaac found himself staring down through a grill into the indoor arena, and into the face of a Jewel dragon.

Isaac froze. The dragon was just inches away. He could smell its foul stench. For one terrifying moment he was sure a fiery red eye had spied him in the tunnel. But the dragon quickly turned away, letting out a blood curdling roar as it prepared to attack Excelsior below. Isaac let out a long shaky breath of air. He must be mad thinking he could help. What did he think he, Isaac Ankama, a fifteen-year-old boy could do?

I can be with you Jo, with you and XL, if nothing else; let you know that you were right and I was wrong – so wrong.

Suddenly he felt the slow prickle of fire over his

skin. Looking down at his hands he saw a silver flame flickering over his fingers.

Armageddon struck Excelsior hard. Joanna didn't want to look, but her eyes refused to leave her dragon as Armageddon gripped him by the neck. He was throttling him tighter and tighter, shaking his body as though it were nothing more than a rag doll. Excelsior's body grew limp and Armageddon released his claws, allowing Excelsior to drop like a stone to the ground. Gathering speed Armageddon prepared to smash down on top of the silver body. She was going to watch her dragon die.

Knowing everyone's attention was fixed on the two dragons, Spiky Mike staggered across the cave floor and yanked the hook out of the wall. He held Joanna tightly to his chest to hide her view. But Joanna pulled away. She would be strong for her dragon and not let him face this alone. She braced herself for the dreadful moment of impact.

'I love you XL, I love you,' she shouted as loudly as she could, sending out every ounce of love to her dragon.

There was a flash of bright light, like lightning, and the next thing she knew Excelsior had rolled out of the way and was suddenly safe up in the air. There was no time for Joanna to wonder how her dragon had escaped. Armageddon howled in rage and blasted out another torrent of sulphurous fire, poisoning the air with choking smoke. Stamping his feet, he leapt back up into the air. Only, instead of chasing after Excelsior, he hovered by the balcony overhang under which Joanna and Spiky Mike were sheltering. He struck the ledge with his tail and a chunk of sharp rock cascaded down, narrowly missing Spiky Mike's head.

Spiky Mike only just stumbled out of the way in time. 'Ebony's cave, Jo. It's our only chance.' He pulled the rope off from around her neck and together they hurried towards the open doors, ignoring as best they could the terrified screams from the balcony. It was a good thirty-five metres across the cave floor. Marius King, standing in front of the main locked doors, realised too late they were trying to shelter in Ebony's cave. Not so Armageddon, who turned to swoop down on his fleeing prey. Claws ready to rip, fiery breath intent on withering human flesh, the dragon prepared to strike.

From above Excelsior pounced on his arched back and, started to breathe a twisting dark grey-blue flame over the Jewel dragon. Armageddon stopped mid-air, momentarily subdued by the feelings of despair and anguish that were overwhelming him. But the effort of maintaining the mood-enhancing fire was taking its toll on the exhausted Excelsior and the flame slowly fizzled out. A renewed sense of fury inflamed Armageddon and he sent Excelsior hurtling across the cave. But Excelsior's fire had given the others the few precious seconds they needed to reach the cave. Spiky Mike started to close the doors.

'XL, here, quick,' yelled Joanna. Excelsior flung himself through the narrowing gap, hitting the far wall. They pulled the doors closed just in time as Armageddon threw his full weight against the ancient timber and began a relentless attack, hammering the wood again and again. The heavy doors creaked, but held firm. In the pitch black of the cave every brutal thump seemed magnified a thousand times.

'We need to get out of here fast. I'm not sure how long these doors will last . . .'

Spiky Mike's voice was shaking,. 'The other exit to the passageway must be . . .'

He found the handle in the darkness. It was locked. They were trapped.

Spiky Mike fumbled at the wall and the emergency lighting came flickering on. As soon as he had untied Joanna's hands, they both turned their attention to where Excelsior lay in a crumpled heap at the bottom of the cave wall. His eyes were open and his wings were twitching uncontrollably. Joanna flung herself down next to him.

'XL, XL . . .'

'JoJo, my front right leg, I can't move it . . .'

'Let me see, Jo,' Spiky Mike bent down and examined it. 'I don't think it's broken, just badly bruised. Can you take your weight on the other legs?' Excelsior staggered slowly up. 'What about your wings?' Excelsior winced as he slowly unfolded a wing. There was a deep rip along the edge so that a flap of skin hung down.

'And the other?' The other wing was similarly damaged. Spiky Mike looked grave. 'They need stitches.'

'Doesn't every cave have an emergency stun gun?' said Joanna suddenly. 'You know Sir John Miller safety regulations and all that.'

'All Ebony's equipment is down in Brighton,' replied Spiky Mike despondently.

Joanna looked up him, her eyes suddenly hopeful. 'But there's a spare one in Vincent's study . . . and I can get to it through the air-duct tunnels.'

Spiky Mike didn't like the suggestion one little bit.

'What if you get stuck or lost?

'I've been in them before,' Joanna admitted reluctantly. 'I followed Hermes one time.'

'But how will you get up there?'

She put her arms around Excelsior's neck.

'XL, I know you are in terrible pain, but can you fly just as high as the air duct?'

Spiky Mike shook his head. 'If those wings rip any further . . .'

'If we don't stop Armageddon it won't make any difference,' said Excelsior softly.

Isaac watched in horror as Armageddon hurled his weight against the doors, gouging out huge splinters of wood with his razor-sharp claws. How long before the door collapsed? Then there would be no place to hide. Isaac's attempt to make the silver fire had saved Excelsior briefly, but he needed to get closer. He shivered and looked back to where he could just make out Hermes sheltering in a small alcove behind him. 'Can you do it?' he asked. 'Can you fly me down . . . there?'

He felt Hermes squeeze up beside him.

'Ready when you are!' said the golden dragon.

This time Joanna knew to expect the pitch-blackness and the echoing sounds. From every direction she could hear Armageddon's relentless battering as he attacked the door. The tunnel was actually vibrating under her hand. She had to hurry. She crawled on to the first junction of the tunnel, knowing she had to take a left. She crawled on. Where was the next opening? Suddenly she felt the change of air and an opening to her right. *Please let this be the one* she whispered desperately to herself. The tunnel went on for what seemed eternity. Had it taken this long before?

And then her hand touched the wire mesh covering. To her relief it gave way easily and tumbled to the floor below with a clatter. But how was she going to get down? It was pitch black in the study and she didn't fancy falling headfirst. She had to turn round and let herself down feet first. In the end she crawled back to the turning and then reverse crawled back again. Oh why hadn't she thought it through more? She was wasting valuable time.

It was lucky that she did land feet first for she heard the crunch of glass as she landed. She made her way carefully over to what she thought was the desk to find the lamp, only to bang her arm on the leg of an upturned chair. She staggered over to the wall and carefully felt her way in over to the main light switch. One flick revealed the complete destruction of Vincent's study. Glass test tubes and flasks lay shattered and broken. Book covers and torn pages lay half-burned in the grate. The desk had been overturned, the drawers smashed, their contents trampled. Vincent's chair had been slashed. How would she find the stun gun in all this chaos?

Think this time, Jo she told herself. *And don't cry.*

She so badly wanted to just sit down and burst

into tears. Spiky Mike . . . XL . . . her family . . . everyone in the balcony . . . they were all depending on her finding the stun gun. Where would it be? She hardly went in to Vincent's study these days as Mr Hogan always had some experiment set up. If only Isaac were here – he knew the room inside out, even in this state. Wait, Isaac . . . A memory flashed into her head – Isaac jokingly putting the gun in the umbrella stand by the door. There was an upturned chair in the way and a large wooden box full of papers dumped on top. *Please be there.* Joanna pushed everything to one side and . . . there was the stun gun! Even better than that, it was fully loaded.

'Thank you, thank you thank you,' she shouted out loud. The desk was nearly too heavy for her to turn upright, but eventually she managed to push it into position under the air duct and she climbed up. Taking a deep breath, Joanna slid the gun into the tunnel and pulled and wriggled herself back into the dark. She stopped and listened. Why was it so quiet? And what was that smell of burning?

33
THE SILVER
FLAME

Back down in Ebony's cave, Spiky Mike was frantic with worry. Excelsior was lying along the wall of the cave. He was too injured to put up much more of a fight. Where was Joanna? Had she found the stun gun? It was their only chance. He stood underneath the air vent, yelling Joanna's name. He'd almost given up hope when there she was, a small white face peering down.

'Catch!' She held out the stun gun and dropped it down into Spiky Mike's waiting arms.

'Stay where you are Jo, but if this all goes wrong, get back down the tunnel and get out of here,' ordered Spiky Mike.

Spiky Mike threw off the safety catch, and aimed the stun gun at the door. It was seconds to go now. He could see the flames. He was frightened, more frightened than he had ever been in his whole life. He thought of Afra. How much he loved her. He hoped he'd see her again . . .

He heard a thud and one of the doors crumbled beneath the blow. Armageddon came charging towards him in a cloud of smoke and flame. Spiky Mike fired straight at the dragon, one straight between the eyes, three more, one after the other, into its belly. Wasn't that enough? He kept on firing . . . the darts were just bouncing off the dragon's armoured skin . . . Armageddon was too close . . .

To Joanna, hiding in the entrance to the air duct everywhere was fire and smoke. She felt the crack of a tail striking hard rock and an angry roar resounded through the cave. Below her Excelsior cried out. She couldn't hear or see Spiky Mike at all. Why wasn't the stun gun stopping Armageddon?

All of a sudden bright silver light exploded through the cave, dazzling Joanna. She couldn't see. All she could hear was the sound of Armageddon crashing into a wall. Of someone screaming. Slowly her eyes started to make out shapes in the cave below, still glowing as though it were on fire. Armageddon was staggering back to the door of the cave, his tail still thrashing lethally from side to side. The smaller shape of Excelsior cowered against the wall. And there was someone else. Isaac, lit up in the light of burning sulphurous fire, was running across the cave. . .

'Isaac!' She forced herself to shout his name. 'Isaac!'

Her voice was drowned out by an almighty crack. The rock wall around the burnt-out door was giving way. A massive shard of rock came crashing down on top of Armageddon. She saw him fall, his skull crushed by the weight of rock. He had to be dead – he must be.

Joanna waited and waited for Spiky Mike or Isaac to shout, for XL to speak to her. But nothing happened. From her hidey-hole up in the rock wall all she could see was rubble and dust. The only thing she could hear was the thudding of her own heart beating in her chest.

'Isaac? Spiky Mike? XL?'

She called out their names again and again. Why didn't they reply? She began to panic. She didn't want to be the only one left alive . . . She had to get down and see . . . But how? She let out a giant sob, not knowing was worse than anything. And then suddenly there was Hermes beside her in the tunnel. She didn't know whether to laugh or cry. Three wing beats and she was safely down beside Excelsior. He groaned as he opened his eyes.

'Don't worry about me. I'm fine. The others, help the others.'

And then Joanna was running across to where

Isaac, covered in dust, was helping Spiky Mike to his feet. She flung herself on the pair of them.

'You're alive! Oh you're alive.' Joanna couldn't stop crying. Spiky Mike just stood there stunned. 'Isaac! Where did you come from? I've never been so glad to see *anyone*!'

Isaac said nothing. He was trembling all over. He broke away from Joanna and climbed out of the cave, past the body of the dead dragon and out into the vast space of the large flying cave. They followed him out. The balcony was in pandemonium. All the spectators were shouting and screaming at Julian Penhaligon to open the locked balcony door. He was sitting on the top rocking from side to side, and of no use to anyone.

Marius King was lying in a pool of blood, in the centre of the cave. His clothing shredded and mangled. His hair was burned away and large blisters covered his face, which twisted and twitched as he gasped for breath.

'He's still alive.' Joanna stared in horror.

'I suppose we should call an ambulance?' said Spiky Mike, not moving.

Isaac came and stood by Joanna's side. 'Marius King saw me fly down on Hermes. He went wild and started screaming at the Jewel dragon to blast me with fire. The dragon sent out this spray of flame that caught Marius King full in the face.'

'Help.' Marius King's voice was barely a croak. His eyes stared up at them blankly.

'He can't see,' said Isaac.

'You . . . boy?' Marius King called out. 'Save me . . . I'll make you rich . . .'

A strange guttural sound spluttered from his mouth. He gasped heavily and fell back unconscious.

Isaac looked at the others. 'What do I do?'

'You think we should save him?' asked Excelsior in disgust. 'He tried to *kill* us! He killed Vincent. He killed Aurora.' The dragon turned away. 'I can't bear to know he's still here.'

'Vincent would save him, I know he would,' said Isaac automatically. He looked around the cave at all the destruction. 'We should hate him after all he's done, but then we'd be like him. And he'd have won. Don't you see? We have to be better than Marius King. We . . . I . . . have to try and save him.'

Joanna nodded her head, but didn't move.

Isaac took Joanna's hands in his. They glowed softly silver at his touch.

'But first I need to say – I'm sorry I didn't believe you and I'm sorry I lost my temper with you and ignored you. Jo . . . I make the fire because of *you* . . . I love . . . *you*.'

Despite the wretchedness of everything, Joanna could only smile.

'Not Amber?'

'Not Amber.' said Isaac determinedly. 'And Jo, I have to do this. The *Alchemist* has to do this. It's who I am.'

He held out his hands, silver flames curling around his fingers. As he knelt down beside Marius King the fire leapt from his hands and flickered up and down and over and around the motionless body, growing in brightness and intensity. Suddenly Isaac jumped up as if he'd been given an electric shock. Marius King was on fire. He was burning up . . . disappearing before their eyes . . . disintegrating . . . until all that was left was powdery grey ash.

Isaac shook his head in disbelief.

'Mr Hogan told me once that the silver fire burns away all the impurities. There must have been no goodness left in Marius King, none at all. All his dreams and ambitions corrupted into hate. And now he's gone.'

Isaac looked around at the others.

'I should be glad, so why do I feel so incredibly sad?'

That was the moment the police stormed the caves. All Joanna could recall after was lots of hugging and crying, warm blankets, tea, Isaac next to her holding her hand and Excelsior at her side.

34
JOANNA MAKES
A DECISION

It made sense to move down to Brighton. The Brixton caves – *her* caves were out of bounds for the time being. Already the structural engineers had made emergency repairs to the rock wall that had collapsed on Armageddon to stop it from collapsing further.

'I've been told the caves will be fine, but the full repairs are going to take months, not weeks,' Anthony Morris told his daughter.

He'd just returned from the emergency trustees meeting. By the end of the week the Brixton team had decamped to Brighton completely – along with the dragon eggs, trophies, Joanna's school books, office equipment and what little was left of Vincent's treasured books on alchemy.

'I suppose we're lucky to have somewhere to go,' Joanna admitted to Excelsior. 'And by the sea, too.

I'm sure it's the air that's helping your wings heal so quickly and Isaac's promised he'll make the silver fire so that there's no scar tissue. How does Ebony like having you and Hermes for neighbours?'

'Poor Hermes, he's too big to escape through the air vents now. And Ebony's much chattier these days. A chap can hardly get a word in edgeways. But it's nice having company.'

Ebony had finally revealed the terrible secret that had held her in such a state of fear for so long. Hannibal listened in disbelief.

'My sister, Jet, was ill. Jamie Penhaligon misdiagnosed it and she died. He should have been struck off for such a careless decision, but he came to some arrangement with Cliff Heywood to hush it all up. Dr Penhaligon threatened to kill me if I even whispered it to anyone and I believed him.'

Both Julian and Jamie had been arrested and charged. Marion Claverdale came down to Brighton to give detailed news. Julian's involvement was purely down to money. He was bankrupt and desperate to keep the Tintagel Caves. His only plea was that he had believed he was part of a research project and that fighting dragons (under controlled circumstances of course!) would be good for business. Once involved with *Dr Braithwaite* there was no going back. He had pleaded guilty and in return for a lesser sentence had revealed all his contacts, including Cliff Heywood. As for Jamie's involvement – the price of Cliff Heywood's silence over Jamie's misdiagnosis of Jet had been that Jamie would care for any injured dragons and ask no questions.

'What about Amber?' Joanna had asked.

She'd thought about her quite a lot over the last few days.

'Amber won't be charged. We all know how easy it is to be taken in by Marius King. However, she will not compete in any more races this season. After that depends on whether or not she wishes to continue to race. By the way, she asked me to return this to you, Isaac. It was found down in Tintagel, in Marius King's belongings. She passed a brown envelope across the table.

Isaac took out a thin battered book. There was a handwritten note too. It said one word: *Sorry*.

So Joanna had been right – Amber had taken the book. He slid the book across the table to Mr Hogan.

'I think you were looking for this.'

Mr Hogan's eyes nearly popped out of his head and he let out a cry of delight.

'Not *Liber Elementorum*!' He wheeled his chair towards the door, saying 'Please excuse me but I am going to make a copy of this book right now. Isaac we can try another experiment this evening! Bring Joanna!'

Joanna and Isaac smiled at each other. Isaac had to be in Brighton to turn the eggs so now they had their lessons together in one of the new classrooms.

One afternoon in late January Spiky Mike came into the classroom. Two faces she recognised trundled in after him. Joanna jumped up excitedly.

'Mouse? Dominic? What are you doing here?'

'Applying for a place at the school for September, what else?' laughed Mouse. 'We've got our interviews today. I did leave you a message, and an email and I sent you a text this morning. Or are you a bit preoccupied at the moment?' She looked deliberately at Isaac, who grinned back.

'Phones are switched off in this classroom,' interrupted Mr Hogan.

Joanna suddenly had a vision of sitting in class with Mouse and Dominic and Isaac. She turned to Spiky Mike.

'Can anyone apply to come to your school?' she asked.

'Of course,' said Spiky Mike. 'Why? Do you know someone who wants to come? The deadline for applications is next week.'

'How about . . . me?' Joanna looked cautiously up at her trainer.

'What about Brixton? The repairs will be complete by summer. I thought you'd want to be back as soon as possible.'

Joanna hesitated. 'I do . . . but my friends will be here, and you should be here with Afra. And I really like what you've done to the caves and perhaps we could do something similar in Brixton . . . so that when I leave school . . .'

'We can all come and live with you in Brixton – perfect!' said Mouse, finishing off her friend's sentence for her.

Spiky Mike looked hard at Joanna. 'Is it what you really want? Do you want time to think about it?'

The more Joanna thought about it the more she knew it was the right thing to do, but first she had to speak to Excelsior. To reach his cave she had to walk past the memorial plaque commemorating Vincent. It reminded her just how inextricably linked the histories of both the Brixton and Brighton caves were.

'What do you think, XL?' she asked her dragon. 'Are you happy to be here for the next four years?'

The silver dragon breathed deeply. 'Wherever you are, I am happy.'

'I hoped you'd say that. I'll tell Spiky Mike it's a yes, then.'

Joanna didn't leave though, but stayed sitting next

to her dragon. Isaac found her still sitting there when he came to feed Excelsior.

'Are you OK?' he asked. He sat down next to her and she put her head on his shoulder.

'I've decided,' she said. 'I'm going to train here in Brighton.'

'I'm glad,' said Isaac. 'It will be fun being here with Mouse and Dominic . . .'

'And you,' said Joanna, wiping away a tear.

'So why are you sad?'

'I'm not sad, really. It's just that it's the end of . . . something special.'

Isaac turned her face to his and kissed her.

'This isn't the end,' he smiled. 'It's just the beginning, JoJo Dragon Flyer!'

Find out how it all began for JoJo and Excelsior in
the first two *Dragon Racer* adventures . . .

*The dragon's face was so close Joanna could feel its
hot breath on her cheeks. She reached up to touch it . . .*

Joanna Morris has no idea that her life is about to change
once she shoots to stardom as the youngest dragon flyer in
the country. Flying the stunning Silver Spiked-Back racing
dragon, Excelsior, is more exciting than anything she's ever
known and he's soon her closest friend in the world.

But beneath the glitz and glamour of dragon racing
lie burning ambitions that threaten to consume anything
and anyone that stands in their way – including
the sport's rising stars . . .

Also published by Catnip . . .

Loser in one world, hero in another.

Edwin Spencer has enough problems at school as it is,
without strange voices calling him into another dimension!
But when he is sucked into the peculiar kingdom of
Hysteria on a secret mission he feels very at home. This
could be his chance at last to be a hero, even if he does
have Perpetua Allbright, school swot, as his sidekick.

You can find out more about Joanna and
Excelsior and the world of dragon racing at:
www.jojodragonflyer.co.uk

For more information on other
great Catnip titles go to:
www.catnippublishing.co.uk